TIME
TILTER

For further information, contact:
Tumblehome Learning, Inc.
201 Newbury Street, Suite 201
Boston, MA 02116, USA
http://www.tumblehomelearning.com

Ellis, Sonia
TimeTilter / Sonia Ellis - 1st edition

ISBN 978-1-943431-31-1
Library of Congress Control Number 2017953378

1. Children - Fiction 2. Science Fiction 3. Mystery

Front Cover Designer: Andrea Beaghton
Back Cover Designer: Evanleigh Davis

Printed in Taiwan

10 9 8 7 6 5 4 3 2 1

TIME TILTER

SONIA ELLIS

TUMBLEHOME l e a r n i n g, Inc.

To my sons, Andrew and Jamie:
wherever you are,
that's where I find home

PART I

DELUSION:

a false belief that doesn't change even
in the face of contradictory evidence

THE GIRL IS BEING HANDED TO ANGELIE LIKE A GIFT.

THE OTHERS—SO MUCH WORK. THE FINDING AND CHOOSING. THE MARKING AND TRACKING. THE TESTING OF WHO IS MORE LIKELY TO ENDURE AND WHO IS MORE LIKELY TO FADE AND PERISH.

THIS ONE IS DIFFERENT. ANGELIE SUSPECTED IT THE FIRST TIME SHE SAW THE GIRL WITH HER GOLDEN DOG. AND NOW, TONIGHT, ANGELIE KNOWS IT FOR SURE: THE GIRL IS A SURVIVOR. SHE IS BATTERED, HEAD TO TOE. NOT JUST ON THE OUTSIDE—ON THE INSIDE TOO. THAT MUCH IS CLEAR. SLUMPING, SIGHING, LIMPING...BUT NEVER STOPPING.

THIS NIGHT IS PLAINLY, FOR THIS GIRL, THE LOWEST OF TERRIBLE LOWS. SHE COULD HAVE CALLED SOMEONE, KNOCKED ON A DOOR, EVEN WAVED DOWN ANGELIE'S CAR—THOUGH ANGELIE WOULDN'T HAVE STOPPED— TO ASK FOR HELP. SHE DIDN'T. SHE STAGGERS ON, SET ON HER MISSION, AS A SQUADRON OF ONE.

SHE IS TOUGH ENOUGH. IF ANGELIE WERE TO PUT HER THROUGH THE TEST, RIGHT NOW, SHE WOULD SHOW HERSELF TO BE EXACTLY WHAT THE PROGRAM NEEDS. WHY WAIT ANY LONGER? WHY TRACK MORE AND OBSERVE MORE AND BE CAUTIOUS? THE GIRL, HURT AND ALONE, SURELY HAS NO ONE TO MISS HER. OH...IT'S EASY, SO EASY, FOR ANGELIE TO CONVINCE HERSELF OF THAT. BECAUSE, THE TRUTH IS, ANGELIE IS RUNNING OUT OF TIME. SHE HAS BEEN TOLD—NO, ORDERED—TO FIND ONE MORE SUBJECT. IF SHE DOESN'T—WELL, SHE CAN'T EVEN THINK IT. THAT ISN'T AN OPTION.

ANGELIE MAKES UP HER MIND. JUST LIKE THAT, SHE ACCEPTS THE GIFT.

Chapter 1
Singer

"Who throws away a dog likes he's nothing more than garbage? Who is *that* heartless?"

I don't have the nerve to say the words out loud, right into my parents' faces. But those are the questions thumping in my head as Mom hands Dublin's leash over to Mr. Winter, the owner of the West-End Salvage Yard.

"He can't compete anymore," Dad explains to Mr. Winter. "So we don't have any use for him. Not with that injury." He nods toward the jagged scar running down Dublin's left shoulder. "And now that he bit a trainer...well, I can't trust him anymore."

"If he bites, he's welcome here," Mr. Winter says. "I'm getting sick of the break-ins but I can't be here round the clock. A guard dog could help." He loops Dublin's leash around one weathered hand and with the other gestures toward the salvage yard, which is a mile-wide dump for wrecked and rusty cars surrounded by a chain-link fence. "I'll put him in the yard at night."

Dublin strains against his collar, his brown eyes wide. I want to rush to his side, sink down beside him and tangle my fingers in his fleecy fur. I want to yank the leash out of Mr. Winter's hand, unclip it from Dublin's collar and lob it over the fence. Dublin has never needed a leash. He wants to be close by whether you ask him to or not.

I can't even believe I'm here, witnessing this.

Just twenty minutes ago, Mom and Dad picked me up from my weekly appointment with Addie, my physical therapist. Dublin was in the car with them. When he saw me, his backend fishtailed crazily. I slid onto the backseat beside him and laughed, stupidly not even asking why he was there. Dublin hadn't been on any car rides since he stopped competing. It must have felt like a treat to him. And I was just as clueless. After all, Dublin had become sort of a family pet. And didn't family pets sometimes get to ride along on Friday afternoon errands?

So we dropped a few bill payments off at the post office, picked up a gallon of one-percent milk at the market—and oh yeah, wait, there was one more thing on the to-do list: throw the dog away at the West-End Salvage Yard.

Here on the gravelly driveway, I take a step toward Dublin but I'm slow, as always, with my own dragging leg. Mr. Winter is already striding toward his pickup truck. He opens the tailgate and hoists Dublin in before I can take three more steps.

I hear Mom and Dad getting into the car, the engine thrumming to life—all signals that they really mean to go through with this, really mean to leave Dublin behind.

"You can't—you can't just—" A hiccup of air dams up my throat. I stretch one arm toward Dublin and one toward my parents, as if I could somehow pull them together. But everything in this space, in this moment, is spiraling out of my reach.

At the sound of my voice Dublin has started another one of his uninhibited dances. He spins and barks, one sharp call after another.

"Singer, get in the car," Mom says. "You're just making it worse."

I look back toward Dublin. He's a perfectly gorgeous golden retriever. That's what most people see at first. He has orangey fur that makes me think of New England autumn leaves. He's sturdy, with a big blocky head—not the lithe and lean body you'd expect from an extreme sports competition dog. His eyes hold a kindness that makes total strangers want to say hello and pet him. But now all I see is his confusion. His big tufted paws scrape and slide on the metal bed of the truck.

I don't want to yield an inch of ground to Mom, but she's right about this: by standing here I'm making the situation harder on Dublin. As long as he sees me, he'll keep trying to get to me.

Swallowing hard, I make myself do the one thing that seems most completely wrong: I turn my back on Dublin and get in the car.

I twist and stare out the rear window as we roll down the driveway away from the salvage yard, away from Mr. Winter with his worn hands and his desire for a dog that bites. Long after Dublin is out of sight, I stay turned away from my parents. I don't want to see any part of them, not even the backs of their heads.

"Why are you doing this?" I ask.

I didn't intend to say it loud enough for anyone to hear, but the car is small and my words carry to the front seat.

"We've already sunk a bunch of money into his surgery and his leg isn't improving," Dad says. "I know you liked having him around the house, but you're not the one paying for his food and the handlers and the vet bills. If he can't compete, we're done."

I don't really need this reminder. I already know the house

philosophy. On a poster it would look like this: a runner crosses a finish line with her hands in the air and above her is a chunky-lettered message that says *"WINNING IS EVERYTHING."* Both Mom and Dad compete in triathlons, go rock climbing up sheer cliffs and ski impossibly steep mountains. And they want to be the best at whatever they do.

Dublin *was* the best. My parents trained him—and all their other golden retrievers—to compete with them in human-plus-canine extreme sports. Dublin was light-footed and fast, and he teamed with Mom and Dad to win a ton of trophies and ribbons. Those days are over now. At the end of a mountain-run competition, Dublin slipped and slammed his shoulder into the edge of a boulder. There's a video of it online that I watched only once. That was enough to leave an ugly image that I can't get out of my mind: Dublin crashing, flipping and ending up crumpled on the ground.

Up to that day, Dublin was a "very expensive asset" to my parents. So he got a very expensive surgery, and after that they brought him into the house instead of the kennel so they could keep an eye on him while he recovered. Except they weren't really around much to do that, so the job fell on me: changing the dressing on his wound, moving his water bowl into reach, helping him hobble to the back yard. The first time Dublin rose from his bed to greet me when I got back from school, the coldness in the house drew back a little.

"Singer, wake up back there." Dad has parked the car in the driveway, and he and Mom are already out of the car. I follow them into the house, still doing my best not to look at them. When we get through the front door there's no bark, no clatter of claws, no happy dance just for me.

It's dinnertime, but I'm not in the mood for that. I want to get to my room as fast as I can. I have to navigate the stairs, my left leg slowing me at each step. All the way, I'm under the gaze of six proud and watchful golden retrievers. They're staring out from photographs that line the wall going up the staircase. Vienna, Tokyo, Vancouver, Chicago, Geneva and Dublin...that's my Mom's thing, to name the dogs after cities. All of them are posing with displays of ribbons fanning out in front of their paws. Mostly blue ribbons, but a few second-place reds and third-place yellows that I'm surprised were even allowed into the pictures. When I get to Dublin's photo, I stop. My leg is throbbing worse than usual. Even with his own injury, Dublin had gotten into the habit of going up the stairs with me, positioning his broad back under my left hand for me to lean into. The memory squeezes my stomach and makes my eyes water.

I stumble the rest of the way to my room. Everything hurts: my body from physical therapy, my heart from losing Dublin. The ache is so bad, stretching me so taut, I feel like I'm going to snap.

Which, I'm completely sure, is what happened to Dublin.

He bit one of his trainers, it's true. A couple of months after Dublin's surgery, she took him away for the day, to reintroduce him to some trails and obstacles and make sure he wasn't afraid of them. But she must have pushed him too hard. He must have been in pain. That's the only way Dublin would ever bite. He's just like me that way.

What is Dublin doing right now? Shivering behind the chain-link fence? Barking as loud as he can, thinking he can call us back? That won't happen. Dublin's competitive career is over. His chances of winning anything are about the same as me ever being a champion runner, climber or skier; in other words, zero. No more blue ribbons, so Mom and Dad are done with him.

I'm curled up on my bed when my heartless mother knocks once on my door and opens it without waiting for my okay. "I know you're upset," she says. "I know you miss Dublin. But, listen, we were worried he might be dangerous—"

"Mom. Stop." There are a million things I want to say about how ridiculous that is, but instead I roll to my other side so that I'm facing away from the door.

There's a stretch of silence before she speaks again.

"I saved some dinner for you. It's in the refrigerator," she says. Another pause. "We're heading out in about half an hour. So I'll say good-bye now."

I'd forgotten: Mom and Dad are driving Geneva and Tokyo to some big triathlon competition where they're both expected to earn titles. They always drive through the night to avoid traffic. With the realization that they'll be gone for the weekend, I let out a long slow sigh of release.

"Don't mope around while we're gone," Mom adds. "Call and check in with me if you need anything."

I nod. I don't know if she sees that or not. But I won't check in with her. I never do. Why bother, when she and Dad are always too busy to answer. I know how intense and absorbing those competitions are. There was a time when I actually liked being there and watching them.

A minute later, I hear Mom's footsteps on the stairs. The light fades, my room goes dark and my tears dry...but the ache doesn't fade. It just keeps biting deeper.

It's late into the night when I finally slide out of bed.

There's the muddled beginning of a plan flickering in my brain and I don't want to stop and think it through. It's probably ridiculous and unworkable. It's probably hopeless.

It's this: I will rescue Dublin.

Honestly, that's about the sum total of it. I figure I'll just keep moving forward and the next steps will unfold as I go.

Should I wait for morning? No. I ignore the pleas of my sleepy body and ditch that thought right away. One thing I know about this rescue is that it will depend on darkness. On *not* running into Mr. Winter. It has to be now.

I'm sure Mom and Dad are long gone by now, so I don't have to worry about being stealthy. I get out of my room and reach the top of the staircase—and I see it right away. I see what's missing. Dublin's picture has been taken down from the line-up.

"That didn't take long," I murmur to Dublin, though he's miles away. "But don't worry. There aren't any pictures of me around here either."

Just outside the front door, I realize that the air temperature really does drop at night. It's cold. I have my jacket but I won't—I can't—go back for gloves and a hat now. The next step, I remind myself, is to keep going forward, keep moving on. In the garage, my parents' SUV—the one they use to transport the goldens—is gone. I grab the handles of my electric bicycle and maneuver it out the side door. The e-bike is a cheap one that I got off TradeSellorDump.com after saving my allowance for about a year. It's battered and a too-bright shade of red, and it's almost certainly not charged all the way, because I tend to forget that part where you have to plug it in. I'm not much of a judge of distance but I think the salvage yard is about five miles away. Fully charged, on a flat road, the e-bike can take me ten miles. The odds are good enough. Keep moving on.

I twist the throttle and take off. Down the driveway to Briar Creek Road, a left at the stop sign onto White Birch Drive, another left onto Route 10. I glide along, keeping to back roads and side roads. It's dead quiet out here. The clouds are faint grey patches in the sky. Every now and then the clouds part and the moonbeams slice down through the trees. I keep looking over my shoulder as if someone might be following me. I can't help myself—it's just that feeling you get when you're alone at night with deep shadows all around. I give myself a shake. Someone following me—that's wishful thinking. As if there's someone who cares enough to come after me, to call me back home. The thing is, the house I've left behind doesn't feel like a home. Especially now, without Dublin in it.

The road starts a gentle downhill slant. I should let the bike coast to conserve the battery, but instead I give the throttle another twist and pick up some speed. The wind skims my cheeks and weaves into my already unruly hair and I remember that *this*—this exact moment when the asphalt starts to blur—is the reason I wanted the e-bike so badly. I watch the black bars on the digital speedometer arrange themselves into numbers I can never match under my own power. I wonder if this is why pilots like to fly, so they can watch the altimeter measure heights so far beyond their own reach.

And as that lofty thought spins inside me, the front wheel of the bike catches on something I can't see. The bike skids, kicks and tosses me into the air.

I land hard on my side.

As the pain plows into me, I lie motionless and curl into myself. I try to focus on my shallow breath: inhale, exhale...inhale, exhale. It's so still all around me. I'm on the edge of the road, I think. The thick layer of hurt doesn't insulate me from the hard cold of the asphalt and the midnight air. My hands start to shake and the darkness deepens. The fall has knocked everything out of me: the joy of the high-speed ride and any remnant of a plan. Just keep moving forward? What kind of a ridiculous idea was that? There is no next step. There's just me, body-shocked and mind-stopped and alone.

Down the road, the e-bike is on its side. Its red metal frame glints briefly under a narrow strip of moonlight. One wheel is twisted back at an unnatural angle, like a broken leg. So my ride is dead.

I look up the hill. That's the way back toward my house and help.

But if I go that way, I'll be doing it again: I'll be turning my back on Dublin.

I get to my feet. I take a step. Fire-bites of pain shoot through my left leg, both shoulders and up my neck. I wobble and nearly cry. Another step. No easier. Another. Worse.

It takes me ten minutes to cover the distance to the bike. I want to sink back down to the blacktop. But this time, I will make myself do the one thing that seems most completely right: I will move forward. Let the next steps unfold as I go.

Maybe that wasn't such a ridiculous plan after all.

When, hours later, I turn onto West-End Road, I don't have to think anymore about where I'm heading. The salvage yard is at the end of the road and it's circled by high spotlights that I saw from a half mile away, guiding me in like dots of light on an airport runway.

I look over my shoulder for the hundredth time. Since I crashed the bike, only one car has passed me. I try to imagine what it would have been like, right when I came up with this sort-of plan, to have pulled out my phone and called a best friend and she would have been right there, following me the whole way and having my back. But I don't have a single friend close enough to call for back-up. You don't have a single *friend*, my brain adds cruelly.

I edge closer to the fence. Inside the yard, the cars hunch together at random angles. Every one of them is smashed and missing parts: windows, tires, rear-view mirrors, bumpers and doors.

"Dublin!" I whisper-shout. Mr. Winter said he would put Dublin in the yard at night. So he should be somewhere close enough to hear me. I reach a hand out to the fence and at that precise moment all the lights go out.

I freeze. When I got here, the office windows were already dark and there weren't any cars parked in the driveway. So it's not Mr. Winter or some employee on the night shift who killed the spotlights. Maybe the lights are on a timer? But why would they go out now? It's still not close to daybreak.

I hunch down low and do a slow scan around me. The moon, now lurking behind some cloud cover, is no help. Even if someone were out there, I'd never spot them now: it's bat-cave dark.

Of course, that means no one can see me either. There's no point in stalling out here. I force my searing muscles to move, keeping one shoulder to the fence line as I look for a way in. The weeds, braided high into the chain links, are as lean and pointy as whips. There's some sort of prickly bush that snags my jeans as I feel my way forward. Every three fence poles, I let myself stop to rest and call softly for Dublin. All I hear is my own breath. There's no sign of any living being around here but me.

I'm halfway around the yard when my hand catches on a jagged metal point. I gasp and pull back. I'm pretty sure I've sliced open my palm.

Yeah, I can feel it: a gash and a wet smear of blood. I'm not one of those "tough it out" people, but right now I don't even care about the bleeding. Something about that metal point has caught my attention. I do a quick and careful exploration by touch. Sure enough, it's what I suspected: someone has cut the fence. The links have been severed from a height of about three feet down to the ground.

This must be one of the break-ins that Mr. Winter mentioned. I offer up a silent thank-you to the delinquents who did this. But I don't find the ready-made opening I was hoping for. Instead, the two edges of the cut have been pulled back together and are held in place with four twists of wire. Time to offer another round of thanks, this time to Mr. Winter for his inadequate repair. With shaky hands I untwist the wires. Then I pull my sleeves down over my hands and force the fence open on both sides of the cut, creating a gap that's just wide enough for me to get through.

I shimmy in on my side. When I'm all the way through, I let out a wobbly sigh and close my eyes. My palm is still bleeding but it doesn't seem to matter. Though I've made it into the salvage yard, it looks like Dublin isn't in here. I think I've known that in the back of my head for a while. He would have heard or smelled or sensed me coming. He would have met me at the gate, tossing his paws up on the chain-link fence and wagging his whole back end.

So where is he? Maybe Mr. Winter owns another salvage yard and is keeping Dublin there. Or maybe he figured out what I already knew: that Dublin is no guard dog, that the bite was a fluke and he's more likely to lick intruders than attack them. Anyway, what would I have done, even if I'd found him? Take him back to my parents? No point to that. After all, there are no blue ribbons in his future. He'd only be thrown away again. And as for going forward, taking the next step—did I really believe that the two of us, girl and dog, could march off on some fantastical journey to find our own home?

I don't think a place like that exists.

When something cold and wet streaks my hand, I jerk upright. For just a second I imagine it's Dublin bumping at me with his cold, wet nose. It's not Dublin. It's starting to rain.

I half-walk and half-crawl to the nearest car that has a full set of doors and windows, slide inside and let the sorrow take me.

Chapter 2
Singer

I wake up choking on black smoke.

The car is burning—this car that I think of as mine because for the past few hours it's been my refuge.

When I found the car, all I wanted to do was crawl in and never leave. Now one word explodes in my head: OUT! I thrash upright and slam my shoulder against the dented car door. Without resisting me, the door swings wide and I drop sideways into the weeds.

My shoulder and hip take the punch of my landing. I roll, feeling every saw-toothed twig and clump of gravel.

I have no sense of where I am as I get my feet under me. The only thing that propels me is a do-or-die desperation to get away from the rocketing heat. As far and as fast as I can.

I make it to the fence where I swivel and stare, my back to the chain link. The rain has stopped but it's still cloudy; no stars and no moon to be my nightlights. But who needs a nightlight when my world is on fire? It's not just the car. It's the whole salvage yard.

The spectacle billowing out before me looks like the setting of an apocalyptic movie. The fire pulses from white to sunburst yellow to ragged orange. I watch as the black silhouettes of cars disappear behind the blaze. A Volkswagen Beetle with its nose smashed flat. The skeleton of a Jeep Cherokee that's been stripped of its hood and doors and tires. And my brief haven, the Chevy Malibu with a busted body and four flat tires. Now they're all just food for the fire.

As the flames do their macabre dance, I hear a rough staccato bark.

My heartbeat bumps up. Was that Dublin? Where was he when the fire started? Probably far from here, wherever Mr. Winter took him, but my panicked brain can't accept that logic. If he *is* somewhere in the yard, the flames will scare him, confuse him, He'll never find a path to safety.

"Dublin! *Dublin!*" I try to scream his name but my throat is as dry as dead leaves. I weave back toward the fire, with some jumbled idea of searching every burning inch of it. That's when it happens: a supernova flare and a sound that's like gunfire—no, louder, like pounding thunder.

My last view of the salvage yard looks like this: fragments of metal arcing through the smoky air and a blown car tire coming straight at me.

Chapter 3
Singer

I'm someplace warm. Cozy warm, not fire hot. I can't open my eyes. But I don't care.

There were hands that dragged me from the salvage yard. A voice I didn't know. I was lifted up and shifted sideways. Later sideways and down. Always with care for every place on me that hurt.

I was out of it for a while, that much I understand. I don't know how long.

Now I'm awake, almost. I don't know. Maybe still mostly dormant. I can't open my eyes.

The seconds seep into me, one and then another and then another.

This must be what a sensory deprivation tank would feel like: all nothingness and no-one-ness. I'm floating in a gap in space-time with no comprehension of up or down or now or then. My brain composes skipping wavelengths of thought to fill the voids. Eventually someone will open up my eyes and let me out.

Until then, there seems to be no very good reason to move.

INTAKE INTERVIEW

Interviewer: Angelie Bonneville
Subject: Singer Sirtaine

NOTE FROM AB:

The subject is in post-operative isolation. Sedation has been lifted. She is now fully awake—ahead of schedule—but in a state of confusion.

Physical status: Extensive abrasions; minor contusions on hips and chest; first degree burns on exposed skin; pre-existing muscle weakness in left leg and arm. Eyes are healing and subject's sight does not appear to be impaired.

Angelie:	You're awake, that's—
Singer:	Who are you?
Angelie:	My name is Angelie. I'm the—
Singer:	I don't know you…who…who *are* you?
Angelie:	We've never met. I'm the one who pulled you away from the fire
Singer:	You…got me out of there?
Angelie:	Yes. You're safe.
Singer:	Where *am* I?
Angelie:	It's okay. You're okay. Lie back down and take a breath.
Singer:	Is this a hospital?
Angelie:	Not exactly.
Singer:	Okay, well, I have to go. I have to go find him.
Angelie:	Who do you want to find? You were alone. Weren't you?

Singer: You're sure you didn't see him? A big gold dog?

Angelie: Oh, the dog. Um…no…I didn't see a dog.

Subject is silent.

Angelie: I'm sorry.

Subject is silent.

Angelie: Here, take a tissue.

Singer: I'm not crying. It's just…my eyes are stinging so bad. The smoke…

Angelie: I know.

Singer: His name is Dublin. He's got to be okay. He might have been there when the fire started. He'll be looking for me, okay? I have to go back and find him. I have to go there now.

Angelie: That's not possible. The salvage yard burned to the ground. It's a crime scene now. They'll be looking for whoever started the fire.

Singer: What? Wait, it wasn't me! You don't think it was *me*, do you? Never mind. I don't even care. I'm going back right now.

Angelie: You've been through a lot—

Singer: Are you a doctor? A cop? Or what? Can you take me back there?

Angelie: Stop. Enough questions. Your dog is dead.

Subject is silent and takes the tissue.

Angelie: You need to listen to me.

Singer: No! You need to listen to *me*! You saved my life. I know. I don't have any right to ask. But I need your help to find Dublin. He *can't* be dead.

Angelie: I understand. What you need is time to grieve. But not now. Listen to me very carefully. We have to get you caught up with the others.

Singer: What oth—

Angelie: No more questions. I'll start with—

Singer: Just one more.

Angelie: …

Singer: Why were you there?

Angelie: Singer, you're exactly the person I've been looking for.

Chapter 4
Singer

When I was born, I'm fairly certain my parents took one look at me and wanted a do-over. Wished they could package me up in a carton and return me to the warehouse, checking the box for "Product Arrived Damaged." Because, like I said, they're used to perfect—and I was not, right from the start. In my first hour of life I had a seizure, all jerking limbs and sideways eyes. They lost it. And that was just the beginning of what was wrong with me.

So when Angelie, who I've never seen before, tells me I'm the one she's been looking for, I give that statement all the disbelief it's begging for.

"Looking for *me*? Why? What does that even mean?"

At a height that must be close to six feet, Angelie has no choice but to look down her nose at me. She puts a hand up to her already sleek hair, smoothing it flatter against her head. Every strand is gathered into a bun on the nape of her neck. Her face is an elegant oval and her jacket looks like chocolate-colored silk. I don't see anything about her that suggests any point of connection with me.

"To best answer that, I'll start at the beginning." Angelie inhales like she's prepping her lungs for a deep dive. "Have you heard of the TimeTilter?"

I shake my head. It sounds like a word out of a sci-fi movie that I would never watch.

"Well, if you were a gamer, or if you *ever* watched the news, you certainly would have." Angelie crosses her arms and begins to pace in front of me, wall to wall with careful steps, as if she's going to measure the distance from the beginning to the end of this story. "The TimeTilter is a gaming site that's based on my invention of a new chemical called the superzeitgeber. It adjusts your biological temporal rhythms to alter your perception of time in the local environment."

She glances over at me without slowing her stride. Her words don't gel together into anything that makes sense. And I don't care enough to try to understand. I can't get my head past a mental picture of Dublin, terrified and hunting for me with the flames rising around him.

"I've lost you already," Angelie says. She sits next to me on the gurney that must have carried me from the ambulance—was there an ambulance?—to here. Now we're nearly eye-to-eye. Close up, Angelie's face is pale with a small, lost-looking nose. And her jacket is way too wide at the shoulders. The nose and the jacket put a crack in her elegance that makes me feel a bit better.

"Here." Angelie hands me her phone. Over my shoulder, she taps on the screen to bring up a news site I've never heard of. She opens a bookmarked page, increases the text size and lets me read.

TimeTilter Opening Announced, But No Tech Secrets Revealed

Collusia Corporation has announced that the long-awaited TimeTilter in-person gaming site will open late next year, according to the company's website.

Developed by Dr. Angelie Bonneville, the TimeTilter made headlines and broke world records as the first crowdfunded venture to surpass $200 million USD. Eager backers made non-refundable reservations to book their TimeTilter experience. Yet little is known about what, exactly, that experience will be.

Collusia has released no images but promises fans that the TimeTilter will be "an adventure beyond anything you can imagine in this time." Gamers must agree to inhale a new and proprietary chemical agent called a superzeitgeber.

I shoot a quick look at Angelie. "Inhale a chemical to play a game?" It sounds pretty far out there to me, but Angelie gives me a simple nod as if there's nothing weird about it. I take a breath and scroll to read the rest of the article.

"Zeitgeber" is a term used to describe an external cue, such as light, that tells your body what time it is and synchronizes your internal clocks. Travelers, for example, can help relieve jet lag by exposing themselves to sunlight when they reach a new time zone.

The superzeitgeber chemical is "a pumped-up cue to your body that completely changes your perception of time," says Monet Jourdain, lead environmental designer for the TimeTilter.

Under the influence of the superzeitgeber, gamers can live through what feels like days inside the TimeTilter, but when they come out, only a few hours will have passed in the real world. That's a huge draw for fans of in-person games. TimeTilter researchers have coined the word Hyperchronicity™ to describe the altered time perception.

The use of a chemical agent to alter perceptions has drawn controversy, but Collusia reports that FDA approval for the superzeitgeber is pending.

Collusia's CEO, Lisa Solein, continues to refuse media interviews and avoid the public eye. That may change with the upcoming, much-heralded opening of the TimeTilter.

My eyes are still burning and watering, so I read slowly, once more to the end and then again. Some of it is confusing, but two things are obvious: one, there's a game you can play where time seems to pass at a different pace; and two, Angelie Bonneville—the same Angelie sitting right here next to me—is a very big deal. So why does she care about me?

I offer the phone back to Angelie. She pauses a few seconds before taking it, holding us both still with a face-to-face stare. I can only imagine what she's seeing: bloodshot eyes, tangled and ash-laced hair, layers of dirt and fatigue. She doesn't wince.

"You holed up in that salvage yard because you were...searching for something. Or walking away from something," she says. It's not a question, so I don't answer. But she's right on both counts. "The place burned to the ground. Whatever you're after, you won't find it there."

Her words fill my lungs like smoke from the fire, making it hard to breathe. But it's true. I have no reason to go back to the West-End Salvage Yard now. All that's left for me to do is go limping back to my parents' house—which I can't, truly can't, bring myself to call home. I try to imagine being there without Dublin to curl beside me and push his broad, soft head against my cheek. The thought makes my chest go hollow. I don't want to go back. But I have no plan now, not even the faintest start of one. I feel like someone has blindfolded me, spun me around a hundred times and left me reeling. I don't see how to move forward.

Angelie nods, as if she sees that conclusion in my face. She rises and gets back to her careful pacing. "I'm going to give you another option."

For the first time since waking up in this place, I take a careful look around the room. Although I'm sitting on a gurney, nothing else in here looks like an emergency room. For starters, I would have expected hospital-grey linoleum on the floor, but instead it's covered with a polished golden wood. The walls are a hazy shade of blue that makes me think of my most faded pair of jeans, comfortable to look at. The framed pictures on the wall look like nature photographs: there's a narrow path zigzagging through a forest, a stream bending past a rough heap of rocks, a row of prickly bushes whose branches are linked like arms. But there's something not exactly real about them. In every one, the colors are a bit too bright and the edges a bit too stark, with some sort of distortion that I can't quite figure out. The air in here is tinged with the smell of smoke and singed skin—which, I realize with a start, must be coming from me.

I shake my head and take in the rest of the room. Chairs with fat pea-green cushions stand in neat lines along the walls—like people at a party waiting for something to happen. Now that I think about it, this space looks a lot like a doctor's waiting room. I've been in enough of them to know. But what would anyone in here be waiting for?

I slide off the gurney, slowly letting my feet take my weight. My body feels like a brittle rubber band that will break if it's stretched too far. I aim for the nearest cushioned chair and totter toward it. Angelie tracks my progress across the floor but offers nothing. If Dublin were here...if he were here, he would glide up and position himself by my side. I'm small for a fifteen-year-old human girl, and Dublin is...no, Dublin was...tall for a young golden retriever dog, so we matched up just right. How did he always know exactly what I needed? The sorrow of losing him digs an ugly cavity into my chest.

I squeeze my eyes shut, tired of fighting the burn and the tears, and crumple into the chair.

"Tell me," I say, "what the other option is."

Chapter 5
Singer

"**W**hat I'm offering you," Angelie says, "is an opportunity that some people would kill for."

I open my eyes to find that Angelie is sitting too, in a chair she's rotated so that we're facing each other. Our knees are nearly touching.

"The TimeTilter, Singer. Do you have any idea how many people want to get in? No? I'll tell you. The wait list is over two years." Angelie smiles for the first time. "This is what I'm handing you, Singer. A chance to jump the line. To get into the TimeTilter ahead of all those gamers who would do just about anything to be you right now."

I'd like to close my eyes again and block her out. Angelie's gaze is too fierce, in weird contrast to her smile. I'm usually good at reading people's faces and judging their moods, but it's not working with Angelie. She's like a car pieced together from salvage yard parts. Nothing fits together in a way that I can recognize.

"So, you're giving me a chance to inhale a chemical and play a game?" I say, echoing my earlier reaction after reading the article on her phone.

"It's not that simple." Angelie gives her chair a little hitch, edging closer. I get the feeling she's not thrilled with my reaction. "I'm giving you a chance to play the game, yes. But the TimeTilter is far more than a game. It's a pocket of time that doesn't follow the rules. It's a place where you can have days upon days of life experiences that cost you no more than a few hours of real time."

"It sounds like you're saying...I'll live longer if I go in the TimeTilter?" Skepticism turns my voice thin and shadowy.

"No." Angelie's hand chops the air inches from my face. I pull back but she leans in even closer. "That's a common misconception that I've been fighting from the start. Here's how I like to explain it: You've got a river that starts here, at Point A. And it ends here, at Point B, where it empties into a lake. So the river is this long, from A to B. Do you see it?"

Angelie has stretched her arms wide to mark the two points. I can sort of see it in my head, a band of cold water sliding along a pebbly grey riverbed. I nod.

"All right. Now imagine a storm. It's raining heavily, for days on end. The river doesn't get any longer, of course. It still runs from Point A to Point B. But the water level rises. The river swells higher and higher."

I let the image evolve in my mind: the raindrops pelting down, the river rolling and arching its back and climbing the banks.

"So now, Singer, imagine that Point A and Point B mark the beginning and end of an hour. Being inside the TimeTilter for that hour is kind of like being in the river during the storm. What the TimeTilter gives you is a chance to take that one narrow sliver of your life and stretch it wide and high. You will perceive a long, rich sweep of time, of experiences—yet when you come out, you still end up at Point B. The end of that one hour."

I wonder briefly if Angelie ever talks to the media. If the TimeTilter belonged to me, I would push her in front of cameras and reporters every day. Listening to her voice is kind of like launching a boat into her river: the current carries you away but the view is so mesmerizing, you don't want the ride to stop.

Then again, there's that stare.

Angelie folds toward me slowly and rests the tips of her fingers on my shoulders. "That's why I chose *you*. I don't believe you want a life that's narrow."

The arrogance of that statement makes my whole body stiffen. How can she possibly pretend she has any idea what I want? After last night, pushing forward step by step, all I know is this: the one thing I want is for time to rewind. To go back to that moment at the salvage yard when Mr. Winter took Dublin's leash. I should have done something. I should have stopped that moment in its tracks. But like always, I wasn't fast enough to grab the leash. I wasn't strong enough to keep fighting and make my parents understand that Dublin, even without his blue ribbons, was worth hanging on to.

Now I'm pinned in this place with an eerie-eyed person who thinks I'm exactly the one she's been looking for, whatever that means. My world has unhinged itself from normal. I have no idea what's supposed to happen next. Every part of me—head to heart to toes—hurts. I didn't realize it was possible to be this bone tired and still manage to breathe.

Angelie begins the effort of another smile, but she doesn't make it past a lip twitch. Both of us turn to the sound of a thwack on the door. Angelie moves quickly: in an instant she jumps out of her chair, enters digits into a keypad, and opens the door just enough for her to see who's on the other side.

There's about ten seconds of low grinding talk before Angelie shuts the door with a smack of her palm and strides back to me.

"We're out of time. We need to meet up with the others."

I blink. The room's edges are shifting and going fuzzy. I've felt like this before, when my pain meds leave me dehydrated. But now it's something else. It's my mind on overload.

Angelie grips my right arm. "It's very simple, Singer. You have nothing to go back for."

I raise my face to Angelie's. The look in her eyes sends me right back to the salvage yard fire. The burnt-orange heat, the spitting crackle...it's in my head again. But as Angelie's anger fills the air, I get the feeling it's not meant for me. It's anger fed by desperation. Angelie needs this to happen, needs me to enter the TimeTilter.

"Are you ready?"

There's a tiny part of me that wants nothing more than to fold. It would be so easy to hand myself over to Angelie, to let her take charge and tell me what to do. But going into the TimeTilter is her answer, not mine. The time in that place might be stretched out and shiny, but it wouldn't be real. I'd have to come out again. And what then? Dublin would still be dead.

That's right. Dublin. His sturdy body against my leg, the soft drop of one big paw on my arm, the brown eyes deep with past pain and present trust, the times when the sound of his breath reminded me that I wasn't alone. So it's not true that I have nothing. I have all those memories. And while I've asked Angelie about what's going on in here, I have even more questions about what happened to Dublin and me out there in the salvage yard. Those, I'm certain, are the questions I need to get answered first.

I step back and Angelie lets go of my arm with no resistance. I turn and head to the door.

"Thanks for getting me away from the fire and for offering me a chance at the TimeTilter," I say. It's my most solemn and formal voice; I sound like I'm at a funeral.

I try to turn the knob and then remember that I can't open the door without the code for the keypad. "The answer is no. I can't go in the TimeTilter. Now, could you please let me out?"

No reply from Angelie. Without meeting my eyes, she points up to a monitor in the far corner of the room. Until now the screen has been black. Angelie picks up a remote control that's on one of the pea-green cushions and clicks a button.

And the video begins to play.

VIDEO EXCERPT

Dublin wakes.

He's on a floor that's shiny and sleek.

He struggles to rise but his legs splay out and he topples to his side, landing with a cruel thud and a yelp. He rises again, more slowly this time, and stands very still. His grip on the floor is wobbly. He doesn't move, not even his head.

Dublin fixes all his attention on the opposite wall and breathes. Time passes unmarked. The breaths turn to pants and his tongue slides out.

The room is empty of everything: no humans, no food, no water, no noise. Empty.

Then comes the sudden high-pitched clang of a latch.

Dublin lets his paws slide and slams to his belly. His ears are arched back, his tail pinched tight to his body. There's no cover in the room and no hope of running to a corner. All Dublin can do is lie flat. And shake.

The wall ahead begins to grind sideways. Dublin tenses. As the opening widens his nose quivers: he must be slammed with scents.

A stretch of glossy, treacherous floor lies in front of Dublin. But he begins a soldier-crawl toward the opening. It's inch-by-inch and it must hurt. With each hunch forward, he leaves behind a feathered smear of blood.

He tries to move faster, but the slippery surface won't let him. When at last he reaches the opening, when his front paws leave the cold floor and touch the yielding soil, he pulls himself forward and — with no sight of where he will land — he leaps.

NOTE FROM AB:

Image uploaded to collusia.com/intake/trial03-subjk9

Chapter 6
Singer

My heart was detonated once before, when I found out Dublin was dead. Now it explodes again, each previous piece crackling into a million more. Not because Dublin is dead...but because he's alive.

"It's real. He's here," Angelie assures me, though I haven't thought to question her. That's how big my need is for this to be true.

"So...why?" I ask. "Why did you tell me he died in the fire?"

Angelie stops the video. She still won't look at me, so she doesn't see my tears or the way my body rocks forward and back, my arms clutched across my chest.

"I thought you needed to know that you had no reason to go back," Angelie answers. Her eyes are as empty as canyons. "Then I understood, Singer, that you needed a reason to go forward."

Sonia Ellis

Singer's Portfolio:

collusia.com/timetiltertesters/singer

Chapter 7
Jaxon

Watching Joy throw a left jab, uppercut and rear leg roundhouse, Jaxon was certain there was nothing on the planet as fierce and as beautiful as Joy in a fight.

"You could *help* me"—she huffed, her black ponytail swinging—"by *holding* this guy" —she threw out a jab, cross, jab—"*still.*"

Jaxon stayed where he was. Safer, here, than in front of those fists and those feet. "You're doing fine. He's knackered."

"Not quite." *Thwunk. Thwunk. Crack-thwunk.* With the last kick, she drove her opponent backwards and flat to the floor. "There."

Joy stepped back and wiped her forehead with one palm. It was September and early morning, which should have meant brisk air. But inside the house, with the windows all boarded up, Joy was sweating. One fugitive strand of hair had escaped the ponytail and clung to her cheek.

The fight was definitely over now. Jaxon pushed himself off his seat—a warped nightstand barely balancing on three-and-a-half legs—and crossed the room to stand over the body. He gave it a poke with his boot. "Better you than me."

The body didn't respond. Which was to be expected: it was a red vinyl punching bag that Joy had dragged up from the basement. At the bottom of the staircase she had also found a rusting can of nearly congealed black paint. She'd dipped her finger in and painted a face on the bag: an X for each eye and a jagged scrawl for the mouth. The act was so unlike Joy that Jaxon had snorted with laughter.

At this moment Joy was smiling too, if only a bit. "Funny you should say that." She put her fists up close to her face, dipped her chin and started toward him.

"Wait. No. No no no." Jaxon grinned as he retreated. "Enough kickboxing for today."

"Get the pads on, please. I need more practice."

Jaxon shook his head. "The heart says yes, but the arms say no."

He slid up his sleeves and held up his forearms. They were covered in bruises of every hue from fresh to fading. "Your so-called pads aren't doing their job."

The pads were stacks of newspapers that he could strap onto his arms with strands of electrical cord they had ripped from a toaster. The newspaper was shredding and the cords usually slipped. But Joy, when in the zone of a twelve-step combination of hits and kicks, had a way of not noticing that.

Joy shrugged and lowered her fists, capitulating more easily than Jaxon expected. Under the shine of sweat on her cheeks, her face looked tired.

Not from the kickboxing, Jaxon knew. More from the three months they had been on the move since leaving the foster home. It was the fourth foster home for Jaxon, the second for Joy. Joy had told him over and over how much she hated that place and everyone in it and had to get out—so many times that he stopped listening. Then, early one morning, she'd really left. She had slid into the big bedroom where he slept with the other boys—two other fosters and a biological son—and woken him up. Not to ask him along, just to say good-bye. Jaxon, who up to that point had been certain there was nothing in the world he cared about, discovered that he did care about seeing Joy. So he had followed her—just like the tail on a horse, as his dad used to say. Out the front door and into the pre-dawn. And down the road without looking back.

From foster home to abandoned house. A neat symbolic journey, Jaxon thought, for two abandoned souls.

He eased back onto the wobbly nightstand. It was Jaxon's favorite spot in the room. From this corner, he could see past shadows and into far angles. Across from Jaxon rested a refrigerator that someone, at some point in the house's dead past, had hauled in from the crumbling kitchen. It was turquoise and had weirdly rounded corners, trademarks of an era too long ago for Jaxon to identify. Besides the fridge and Jaxon's nightstand-turned-chair, the only other furniture was the bare-knuckle frame of a collapsible metal cot. Its hinges were jammed, jack-knifing the cot into a permanent V. Oil-stained slices of cardboard were stacked along the west wall, evidence of a makeshift bed left behind by past wanderers.

Joy, with a low sigh that Jaxon figured he wasn't meant to question, had begun her cool-down routine. She bent double to touch her toes; her thick ponytail flipped forward and nearly grazed the floor. She never missed a day of practicing her moves. Not that they had much else to get in the way, thought Jaxon—other than that every-minute preoccupation with survival.

"Hungry yet?" Jaxon asked.

Joy tilted her head back to eye him. "Always."

"Sure I saw a good million dandelions in the yard. They're edible, I think."

"I'm not eating weeds, now or ever," Joy said as she rose up from her stretch.

Jaxon closed his eyes and exhaled. "I've been dreamin' of a proper fry up...rashers...eggs...white pudding."

"Really? Rashers? Seriously, Jaxon, drop it. Have you ever even been to Ireland?"

Jaxon smiled and let it go. She knew the answer. Still, he figured his one-half heritage and red hair gave him enough license to lay on the Irish.

"We need to go. Today," Joy said.

"To Ireland?"

Joy sighed. "You know what I'm saying. We need to move on."

Jaxon shook his head. "Here we go again. You've been saying that for days. There's no hurry. This is a good place."

"A good place? What's good about it? It stinks. I mean for real; it smells *bad* in here. Like something died and now it's rotting. And we're out of food."

Across the room, Joy finished her stretch. Every window in this room—every window in this house—was boarded over with tired grey planks that didn't quite meet. The sunshine squeezed through, striping Joy with bands of dusty light. When she stepped forward and released her damp curls from the ponytail, it looked like she was emerging from water.

"Selkie," Jaxon said.

"What?"

"Selkie," he repeated. "You look like one. A mythical creature."

Joy narrowed her eyes at him, intrigued, as he had known she would be. "What is it?"

"Seal in the water, human on land."

Joy closed her eyes and Jaxon smiled. She'd be cataloging this one in her mind with all the others she kept there: amaroks and thunderbirds and Valkyries. A memory from the foster home nudged at Jaxon. When the two youngest kids had arrived at the home—a brother and sister, five and six—they were jaded and silent and backs-to-the-wall. Joy sat with them every day, telling stories of her mythical beasts. She gave them each a creature of their own to hold in their heads, a sea monster for one and a fire-breathing giant for the other. And though they didn't exactly come to life, the two had at least started coming out of their room, looking a little less scared.

With his whole focus so firmly in that micro-memory, Jaxon didn't even react when he heard the first explosion.

It came with a pop and a spit, traveling right to left along the wall behind Joy. Her eyes, so peacefully closed a moment ago, widened and fixed on Jaxon. He looked back at her but didn't move. The sound didn't make sense, didn't fit this space or time. They were in a deserted house, ten miles out of town, deep back from a dirt road that led to a dump. No people no cars no noise. He had gotten used to silence.

Then, the second explosion: a throaty bass roar that shook the house and pounded Jaxon to the floor. His eyes stayed on Joy's. She took one lurching step toward him. The wall at her back tilted toward her like a sinking ship. Jaxon opened his mouth to scream a warning, but his voice was pinned to the floor and there was no time no time no time. She didn't even look scared, just startled, and that was his last view of Joy before a ten-foot stretch of plank and plaster settled on top of her with an angry sigh of dust and she was gone.

Chapter 8
Jaxon

His fault. It was Jaxon's fault. He knew this completely as he drew his first breath after the wall fell. Joy was slammed under the wreckage and he was to blame.

Jaxon rose to his knees. The powdery air coated his tongue and lodged in his throat, provoking a jagged cough. Shoulders heaving, he lunged toward the pile of splintered wood and clawed at the debris. Within seconds the shredded nails and glass ripped across his hands and arms, leaving crisscrossing tracks of blood.

Joy Joy Joy—where was she? The wood, the stupid wood, he couldn't budge it. Too heavy. One plank on top of the other in an immovable lattice. And Joy somewhere beneath.

He clawed harder and a fingernail snapped back and away. Jaxon blew out a moan of pain he couldn't stop. He let it grow, let it deepen into a full-on bellow that throbbed in his chest.

Joy had wanted to leave this place. For days she had said so. And he had lagged and resisted, wanting this to be their home for a little while. Wanting the world to get off their backs and give them a little more time. If he had listened...if they had left...his one Joy would not be lying under this mad mound of rubble. His fault, for sure.

Jaxon rose and kicked frantically at the unyielding pile. Fragments of sheetrock shifted and puffed out another cloud of white dust. On the other side of the rubble, the missing wall had left behind a perfect empty picture frame. Sunshine gushed through. The brightness—the view into a velvet stretch of grass choked with lemony dandelions—hit Jaxon like the vilest insult. He stopped kicking and screamed every swear word he knew into the morning light.

Like an answer from fate, help came.

A long grey van jolted up the dirt road that twisted past the house toward the dump. Jaxon's whole body flooded with sudden hope.

Then he bolted. Around the rubble, out the front door, through the tall grass.

"Stop!" He yelled with all his strength, sending the word out like a lasso to loop the van in.

It wasn't slowing down. There was no way he could reach the road before the van passed. But surely, surely, the driver must see him: running and catching himself, dripping blood and tears, and pulsing with desperation.

It couldn't be. The van was speeding up. It wasn't going to stop. The vehicle bounced over a pothole and surged forward.

Jaxon froze. The van lurched on. And then, just as its front bumper reached the driveway from the road to the house, the van turned. The driveway didn't even deserve the name; it was no more than two faint ruts in the ground. But it was like the driver knew it was there. She—Jaxon could see, now, that the driver was a woman—yanked the steering wheel and the van spun left, spewing up a fan of gravel and dirt.

The woman tossed a glance at Jaxon and motioned for him to follow. Jaxon pivoted and ran back toward the house in the van's wake.

Now, from this viewpoint, he could see what must have caught her attention. The house looked mangled. The explosion had blown out the entire front wall and a section of roof. Though the house was tucked back from the road, the chaos was impossible to miss. Maybe she had even heard the blast from further up the road.

The woman slung open the van's door. She ran to Jaxon and grabbed his hands. "You're okay? What happened to—"

Jaxon jerked loose. "This way. Hurry."

Everything that happened next seemed to Jaxon like he was seeing it through a jerky hand-held camera. Images rose and fell, snapped sideways, then blanked out and reappeared as his stomach rolled.

The woman asked no more questions. She ran beside him to the rubble. As Jaxon began to dig, she flicked a thin black hairband off her wrist and wound her long hair into a bun at the back of her neck. Then she plunged into the debris.

"Lift that end. No—over there."

Jaxon couldn't let himself think. He forced himself to focus on the woman's hands as they pointed and hovered and then dove into the rubble like two manic birds of prey. Jaxon, stoked up with adrenaline, found himself shifting piles that must have weighed hundreds of pounds. Yet that was nothing next to the loads that this strange woman dead-lifted high above her shoulders and threw aside. Plank by plank she directed Jaxon where to pull and what to pry loose or shift away. With each piece they cleared, the next one came free faster.

When, together, they pulled up the last ragged plank that covered Joy's body, Jaxon's own body quit.

His eyes still scanned the wreckage, his ears recorded the sound of the woman's voice, and his hands still gripped the razor-edged wood. But none of those sensations made it into his brain. A barbed-wire fence had sprung up inside his head. The image of Joy—smashed and still—was not allowed in.

Jaxon sank to the ground beside her and closed his eyes. He might still be breathing, but that hardly seemed to matter. Time might still be passing, but what was the point? He didn't need time. Let it stop, let it spin, either way it meant nothing now. The passing of time made sense only if it marked change, and nothing could change for Jaxon now. Without Joy things could never get worse and never get better. He would be clenched in this moment and in this pain forever.

Jaxon reached blindly for Joy's limp hand and let consciousness go.

Joy Binda. My joy. Brave and strong.

"Did you know, my dad died when I was 13?" she told me once.

"He was sick for a long time. But he taught me to fight. To take care of myself."

"I can't stay here, Jaxon. I need to fight. I need to go..."

"Jaxon."

"Jaxon."

"Jaxon!"

Chapter 9
Jaxon

"Jaxon!"

The woman's voice forced Jaxon into ugly awareness. He blinked once and then again.

He was slumped on the bench seat in the back of the woman's van. She gazed at him, eyes hard, from the rear-view mirror as she drove.

"Wake up, Jaxon. We're getting close."

The woman. He knew her. He understood, sickeningly, why he knew her—she had helped him after the explosion. But how was he here, in this van, on this seat, as she drove too fast on a highway Jaxon had never seen?

"I'm Angelie," she said. "And you're—"

"Jaxon," he said.

"Yes, I know. I was going to say, you're hurt too. You need help. I'm taking you both to the best surgeon I know."

Jaxon tried to sit upright but every ounce of him felt too heavy. He looked down at his arms and legs. Up to this moment his ripped-up skin and muscles hadn't hurt. But now that he'd looked, the pain snarled up at him and showed its teeth. He couldn't think, much less utter any of the words and questions that clogged his head.

But...what had Angelie said? *I'm taking you both...?*

Joy. Where was she? Angelie hadn't, surely, left her...her body... behind?

"Joy?" He spit the word out.

From the rear-view mirror, Angelie pinched her lips into a smile.

"She's been calling for you nonstop." Angelie jerked a thumb over her shoulder, pointing toward the back of the van.

Jaxon spun in his seat. He had never moved so fast and with so much need. There was one more bench seat at the rear of the van and lying across it, wrapped in a grey felt blanket and buckled in tight, was Joy.

I'm dreaming, thought Jaxon. Because there was no way someone so battered and crushed could be so beautifully alive. But Joy's eyes were open and she looked up at him and for a full ten seconds he couldn't breathe.

He reached to her over the top of the seat and she clutched at his hand. The moment their fingers touched, Jaxon was certain he couldn't let go again. She was alive. Her face smudged with dirt and blood, her hair a spiraling tangle, her arms flecked with cuts and welts, her eyes caught in some weird struggle between exhaustion and wariness...but alive. This is it, thought Jaxon. This is the moment my dad always talked about. When you know, even as you're living it, that something so earth-blinding is happening you'll never forget it. You'll hold onto it and even a lifetime later you'll still see it as plainly as you do now. She was *alive*.

"Angelie told me what happened. After the wall fell," Joy said, as if they were still in the middle of the conversation that had ended with the explosion. Her voice was muted, like she had turned, in fact, into a selkie and was talking to him from under water. Jaxon rose and twisted sideways. With a quick, awkward shimmy he slid into the space between the seats, kneeling down to put his face level with hers.

"She said you flagged her down. And you both pulled that wall off me." Joy squeezed his hand a bit harder. Her breath on his cheek smelled like dust. "Then you carried me out of the house and into the van. Is that true?"

Jaxon was so caught on the sound of her voice that he could hardly take in her meaning. "I don't remember all that. Well, I remember finding you, yeah. That's it, though. Nothing after." With his free hand he folded a trailing corner of blanket under Joy's arm. "I guess I kind of...lost it."

"She said she wants to take us to this doctor she knows, this surgeon. And that you agreed."

Jaxon shrugged. His muddy brain was now determined not to let anything out, as careful as it had been before not to let anything in.

Joy shifted. The movement must have hurt: she inhaled abruptly and went still. "Jaxon, I don't trust her," she whispered.

"What?"

"So we're in her van, right?"

"Yeah."

"What color is it?" she asked.

"What color? The van?" Jaxon drew out the words. The question was weird, and he had a quick doubt that Joy even knew what she was saying. He looked out the rear windshield, as though that would give him the answer. Then his memory surged, taking him back to the aftermath of the explosion. He had stood in the tall grass and waved and screamed for help as Angelie drove toward him in the van. "Um, grey. The van's grey, I guess. Why?"

"That's what I thought. I've seen this van before. I've seen *her* before."

"I don't..." Jaxon shook his head. She was talking too fast and he wasn't following. "Joy...I thought you were *dead*."

Joy cut back whatever she had been about to say. For the first time since Jaxon had taken her hand, she looked squarely at him.

"I thought so too," she said. She let out a small, hitched laugh. "There was that explosion, so loud. I could see your face, and I knew I should run, but I couldn't move. I just couldn't move. And when the wall hit me, it happened so fast. I must have been knocked out right away. But there was that second—that split second—when I was absolutely certain I was going to die."

Jaxon shifted back. He wanted no part of this memory.

"You know what that felt like, Jaxon? It felt like being trapped in a place you'll never get out of. It felt like being back in the foster home."

Joy pulled her hand from Jaxon's and laid it across her stomach as if something hurt. Beneath her fingers Jaxon saw a stain on the blanket that hadn't been there before.

"I'm not going back to that place. Ever." Joy's voice went lower. "And I bet that's where Angelie is taking us."

Without thinking Jaxon eased up and looked toward the front of the van. Angelie was focused forward on the road that was spooling out ahead. He could see the long fingers of her right hand clutched around the steering wheel, as cut up as his own from digging through the rubble. She gave no outward sign that she was watching them or listening. But surely she must be trying to keep an eye and an ear on them.

He squatted back down, dropping his own voice to match Joy's. "Where do you think you've seen her?"

"Driving past the house. A few days ago." Joy sighed, a shaky exhale. Her skin looked clammy. "It's a dead-end road. There's no other reason to be there. She must have been looking for us."

Jaxon shook his head. This made no sense. What did Joy think, that Angelie was a secret agent for the Department of Social Services and had been tracking them down since they'd left the foster home?

"There's a dump at the end of the road," he said. "She could have been going there."

"The dump is closed. She's been watching us, Jaxon. Watching us for a while. How else could she have shown up so fast after the house collapsed?"

"Joy, stop. She's helping, remember? You need to get to a surgeon and *that's* where she's taking us."

Joy pressed harder on her stomach. "Then why aren't we going to a hospital?"

Before Jaxon could answer, the van rumbled into a lower gear and swung into a hard right turn. Crouched low next to Joy, all Jaxon could see through the windows was a steady line of dark pine trees.

"We're almost there, wherever 'there' is," he said.

"We're out of time. We have to get out of here." Joy struggled against the seatbelt. "Help me with this. Unbuckle it. Hurry."

"What on this great green planet do you think you're doing?"

"My plan, Jaxon. I have a plan. We can jump out the back of the van."

Jaxon shook his head. The wet, dark red stain on the blanket was spreading. Beads of pain-sweat gathered on Joy's forehead.

Joy yanked on the seatbelt strap with no strength at all. "I'm doing this, Jaxon. Help me."

"You can't run."

"I can. I will."

"You can't even sit up." Jaxon pulled the seatbelt out of her hand. "This is ridiculous. You're hurt. Joy, you're *bleeding*. So no. Just no. We're not doing this."

The van downshifted again and rocked to a stop. Jaxon studied the floor. He couldn't meet Joy's condemning eyes. There was the slam of a door after Angelie slipped out of the driver's seat, then the grind of footsteps on gravel as she quick-stepped around the van and pulled the back doors wide. The light hit Jaxon's face so brightly and brutally that he could hardly see as Angelie pulled the bench seat flat, unbuckled the seatbelts and slid Joy neatly off the seat and away.

The shuddering handheld camera was back in Jaxon's brain to record every bleak second of what happened next.

He scrambled out of the van. Just ahead, at the end of the drive, he saw a tall building that stretched so far into the distance, it seemed to have no end. There were two wide double-doors and dozens of low windows in no obvious pattern that Jaxon could make out. There were no Emergency signs. If this was a hospital, it was trying hard not to look like one.

Joy was now laid out on a stretcher. She looked faded and ragged on top of the brilliant white sheets. Beside her stood a broad-faced, narrow-shouldered man with a stethoscope around his neck. Other than that one implement, he didn't look like a doctor—no white coat, no scrubs—but, Jaxon thought, what did he know about what doctors were supposed to look like? He had not been to see one since he was five.

"Stop this, Jax. Get me out of here." Joy's voice dragged low. She pushed uselessly against the restraints that held her secure.

The broad-faced man gently rotated the stretcher until Jaxon could no longer see Joy's face. He tipped up the front wheels, then the back, onto a concrete walkway and wheeled Joy to a door that must have been motion-activated because it slid open as they approached. As the door glided shut behind them, Joy's arm fell to one side of the stretcher with her hand palm-up. It looked to Jaxon like some sort of signal. One of hope, maybe: *Take my hand. Follow me. Find me.* Or one of despair: *There is no one now to take my hand.*

Tears brimmed in Jaxon's eyes. He did not move to follow.

Angelie appeared beside Jaxon. "Now I want *your* help," she said. "Let's talk."

Chapter 10
Jaxon

She called it "the deal."

Her name was Angelie Bonneville and she talked so fast that Jaxon could barely keep up with her. She was *not* from the Department of Social Services. But she *had* been watching Joy and Jaxon. She knew they were homeless and hungry and she wanted to help them. In fact, she had chosen them. They were exactly the ones she'd been looking for.

There were more words, so many words that Jaxon had never heard before. TimeTilter, that was one of them—so this was not a hospital at all. It was a place where things happened that Jaxon had never considered possible. It was a place where, according to Angelie, a huge number of people—gamers—wanted to be. To live in time that somehow passed differently, flowing around you, like being on a roller coaster, maybe—and coming out of the TimeTilter must be like getting off a ride, back on the ground like everyone else, but shaky-legged and exultant.

"We're taking care of Joy," Angelie told him. "She was injured quite severely in the explosion. But we're stitching her up and she'll be fine."

Jaxon nodded. His throat felt too dry to let him speak.

"You have a decision to make now," she said, putting a hand on Jaxon's shoulder. "For both of you. Becoming early testers of the TimeTilter...this is an opportunity of a lifetime. And if you don't do this—well, let me be clear. You'll go back to the foster home. The same one that Joy was so desperate to leave."

Jaxon stiffened and dropped his shoulder out of her reach. So Angelie *had* heard Joy's whispers in the van. This was bad.

More than anything else he could imagine, Jaxon wanted Joy by his side so they could face this together. He had already let Joy down twice—first by not getting out of that house fast enough, then by not breaking out of the van. Joy had made it plain that she wanted to get away from Angelie and didn't trust her. He should listen this time. He should tell Angelie thanks but no thanks. But if that meant going back to the foster home? Surely that was the last thing Joy would want.

Ignoring his twisting stomach, Jaxon nodded at Angelie again.

"You'll be going into surgery too. You have to be prepped. You'll be unconscious for just a little while," Angelie said, and Jaxon agreed without caring what this "prep" was or how it worked.

He only knew that he would do anything she asked, sign any paper she put in front of him, sign it in blood if he had to because that, after all, was the deal.

Jaxon's Portfolio:

collusia.com/timetiltertesters/jaxon

Joy's Portfolio:

collusia.com/timetiltertesters/joy

Chapter 11
Monet

"These are some pictures from the inside of the TimeTilter. Don't let anyone know I showed you—or I'll have to kill you. ☺"

Monet Jourdain read her email one more time and made sure the high-res images were attached before she hit Send. Her sister would laugh. She would also be impressed.

At barely twenty-two, Monet was the youngest employee at Collusia, but her work was getting noticed. Angelie Bonneville—wait, make that *Doctor* Bonneville—had hired Monet right out of college. Monet understood why. Her grades were merely okay, not stellar. But she'd earned a double major in environmental studies and landscape architecture. And her designs were *good*. Unique. What had Dr. Bonneville said? "You'll make this place look like something that's never been seen before. That's never even been imagined."

Well, that was happening. The TimeTilter gave Monet five hundred indoor acres to play with. Her latest concept, for the floating sky, was nearly complete. And nearly perfect.

But Monet was not satisfied with "nearly." During her last inspection of the North 25 Quadrant, she'd noted two spots where the sky was too translucent and where, maybe, there was a structural sag—invisible to any eye but Monet's. Still, she couldn't ignore it. *Perfectionist.* She could hear her sister's voice in her head, calling her out for the millionth time. Okay, yes. And wasn't that what had gotten Monet where she was now?

Time for another inspection.

Monet closed up her lab and signed a golf cart out of the garage. The property was so big, it took too much time to walk anywhere. Some employees, like Monet, drove the carts outside the building to get from one end to the other. Some, she'd heard, drove the carts inside, through the halls. She didn't have the nerve yet to do that.

At the North employee entrance, Monet pressed her ID card against the pad and waited for the click and hum of recognition.

And waited.

That was odd. Her ID had never been rejected before. She removed the card and placed it on the pad again.

Still nothing.

Monet pocketed the card and called the security office. Put on hold, as usual. Communication in this company was its weak point.

After five minutes on hold, which she spent peering through the glass doors to see if she could catch someone's attention, Monet gave up. She left a message with security.

Back in her office, Monet studied the photos of a broad sweep of forest. The trees' placement looked a bit too natural. She'd been hoping for something quirkier. Maybe if they resized this hill...let the trees sweep higher...

Caught up in her design, Monet didn't notice until very late in the day that no one had ever replied to her message.

Chapter 12
Singer

The dog standing ten feet in front of me looks nothing like Dublin.

I'm used to seeing him bathed, brushed and shining with all of the gold in golden retriever. This dog has matted fur, muddy paws and hungry eyes. He's covered with a dull coat of desperation.

I barely recognize him. But he knows me. The dog leaps the whole length between us, throws up his paws and greets me with all the weight of his body. I'm down on my backside and we're nose to nose and now I see the Dublin I know. Same dog; he just smells like a discarded car and dirt instead of scented shampoo. I hug him and he stuffs his wet, whiskered muzzle against my neck.

I look nothing like the Singer from the salvage yard explosion. I've had a shower, combed my hair and had my wounds treated and bandaged. After all that was taken care of, Angelie brought me here to reunite with Dublin. I'm in some sort of atrium that's neither inside nor outside—somehow a bit of both. It's a small, enclosed space but there's real grass under my feet. Three of the walls are made of tall arched glass. Outside the glass, skinny grey trees with peeling bark ring the atrium like a tight fence.

I give Dublin a gentle shove back so I can get on my feet. Dublin gives me a sturdy and steady base to heave myself up.

"That was a touching reunion," comes a girl's flat voice from behind me. I turn with a start. The girl—and a boy as well—are standing near the same door I came through. This space is so small I don't know how I missed them before. But my attention was all on Dublin, so I never looked sideways or back. Now, all of a sudden, they seem to take over the room.

They're connected in some way, I can tell: the boy gives the girl an apologetic half smile, like he's ready for her to turn the sarcasm on him. There's careful space between them too. They both look like they're about my age. The boy has sun-fire red hair, the kind of bold color that would make it uber-easy to pick him out in a crowd. His thin, shadowed face is heavily dotted with freckles across his cheekbones. His wide mouth looks like it would be in a full-on grin under less weird circumstances. The girl is taller than me—well, most fifteen-year-olds are. Her face is partly hidden by thick coils of hair that fall past her shoulders. Her eyes are beyond intense: two micro storm clouds that make me want to take a step back.

"We're all here?" Angelie walks into the atrium with a satisfied nod and hard steps on the soft grass. "You've all been prepped. So let's get started."

I knew, coming in this space, that it was time to enter the TimeTilter. I was ready. It was my end of the bargain with Angelie and the reason Dublin and I now stood side by side. But I had expected it would be just the two of us, my dog and me. What are these two strangers doing here?

As if she can read my thoughts, or at least my face, Angelie makes some introductions. "Joy and Jaxon," she sweeps her hand toward the girl and boy, "from the Exploding House of Heartbreak."

She pivots and points at me. "Meet Singer—from the Salvage Yard Inferno." The labels could have sounded mean but Angelie gives us our identities lightly; in some peculiar way I think she's only trying to shake the dark mood from the air.

"And, of course, Dublin," Angelie adds. At the sound of his name, Dublin does a happy-face pant toward Angelie and wags his arching tail. I feel a quick shameful stab of jealousy until I remind myself that Dublin can't help it; it's just how he's made. He's a dog who wants to love everyone. I pull him in tighter against my leg.

"You all know where you're about to go: into the TimeTilter. A place, I should remind you, where a great many gamers would like to be—and would pay a great deal of money, more than you could imagine, for the privilege." As Angelie goes into company marketing speak, the girl named Joy looks steadily out the windows at the trees. For the first time I notice that her eyes, and Jaxon's too, are a bit red and irritated, like my own. Angelie mentioned a falling house. And Jaxon's hands look bruised and scarred. Maybe they were caught in some sort of fire, too?

I focus back on Angelie, who's done with introductions and has moved on to instructions.

"You three will be a team," she says. "You'll go on a journey. It's the simplest of all the games we offer. You enter through the East Portal, and all you have to do is cross the TimeTilter and reach the West Portal. When you get there, the game is finished and you can come out." Angelie smiles mildly, as if she couldn't be more relaxed, we'll most likely be bored and it will all be over in a flash. "Remember this: inhaling the superzeitgeber will put the three of you on a connected time perception. You share that perception only as long as you stay in sight of each other—although, yes, it's okay to blink. If you separate, you'll each start going down a different time perception path. We call it perception failure. So stay together, or you'll lose your connection and be on your own."

Angelie gives each of us a slow and careful scan, as if she's assessing our readiness. "As soon as I'm out of here, I'll release the superzeitgeber."

I already know that's the chemical that will put us into hyperchronicity. But the way Angelie says it—"release the superzeitgeber"—makes it sound like she'll be unleashing a beast on us, and I shiver. "Your best bet is to breathe in deeply. That makes for the easiest transition."

Joy glares at Jaxon like she's burning lasers right through to his bones. "Nothing about this," she says in the same flat tone, "will be easy."

Angelie shakes her head. Her voice, which usually comes out at a fast pace, starts spilling out even faster. "You can't start like this. Come together, all of you. Yes, closer. Right here, in the middle of the room. We have a tradition: players always huddle up before going into the game. Closer, come on, *closer*, arms around each other's shoulders. That's it."

I can't help thinking this is the weirdest of all the weird things that have happened so far; I can tell that Joy and Jaxon feel the same way. But Angelie is so insistent that we join in a loose huddle with her.

Her eyes narrow and her words turn low and clipped. "I have about thirty seconds to tell you everything, so pay very close attention." She takes a deep breath. "If you think there's something strange about how I found you, you are right. If you think there's something strange about the fire and the explosion, you are right. There is more to the TimeTilter than a game. And there is more to Collusia than the TimeTilter. Now *clap*!" Angelie starts clapping her hands together, and the three of us are so mesmerized that we follow suit without thinking. Angelie lowers her head, bringing us all into a tighter ring—and in the back of my mind it registers that the way we're standing here, backs to the wall and clapping like fools, no one outside this huddle can see our faces or hear Angelie's voice. "Someone wants you to stay in the TimeTilter. I am telling you that you should try—very hard—to get out as fast as you can. *Never* stop looking for a way out. High five!" Angelie pops upright and holds up her hand. We each slap it halfheartedly and back out of the huddle. For a moment it's like we've all been hit by a Mute button. The room goes utterly silent.

When Angelie speaks again, at a normal volume, her voice fills the atrium. "Like I said, there's only one rule you absolutely need to remember. Stay together. If you go down your own perception path, no one else will be able to see you."

With that she backs out of the door and latches it firmly shut behind her.

I should be turning to Jaxon and Joy, asking questions, trying to figure out what just happened. But there's no time. The "release" of the superzeitgeber chemical begins. From somewhere beneath the floor, a fan ramps up. The air turns cold.

Mist shoots into the room and unfurls around us.

I inhale deeply and then keep my breaths as shallow as possible. Already the mist has completely filled the room and is settling on my skin with a soft glisten. It's entering my pores and my lungs and my bloodstream and my brain. I look down at Dublin and as always he's staring up at me. I lean into him and this time he sinks under my weight. We both fold gently to the floor. The analytical part of me understands that the mist is laced with some sort of anti-anxiety inhalant, along with the superzeitgeber. It's working fast.

Jaxon is still on his feet, but he's leaning back against the wall. His arms are folded across his chest and his face has taken on a day-dreamy softness.

I try to watch Dublin's tail, a golden plume that swings back and forth in a lazy rhythm. It takes every bit of my energy to focus on just that one thing, but I lose track of the motion as my sight begins to fade.

A starburst of color flashes in my brain—no pain, just pure euphoria. I am rising, rising, rising. I am a hot-air balloon cut from its tethers.

I am the crest of a wave that will never break.

I am a dancer who doesn't answer to gravity.

Then the euphoria is gone. And my world is a heavy and coal-black sleep.

Chapter 13
Singer

I'm standing on a cedar-wood platform that juts out over a small marsh.

I'm not completely sure how we got out of the atrium to here. I woke up feeling a bit hollowed but okay. One of the tall arched windows opened like a door, and the four of us—Joy, Jaxon, Dublin and I—went through. It's fuzzy, but I think it was that simple.

The marsh is glutted with tall cattails. I feel a mild breeze at my back that's brushing the tips of the cattails. Across the marsh, a grassy bank rises and quickly turns to forest.

"Angelie said this place used to be a warehouse. One building, five hundred acres," Jaxon says quietly. He's standing near me on the platform. His face, in profile, looks like the rough-cut edge of a cliff. "It's hard to believe."

Something in his speech is different from what I'm used to hearing. Is that what an Irish accent sounds like? Or Scottish?

Either way, he's right. We're inside a building but I swear, from here, it seems like it goes on forever in all directions. There's a ceiling somewhere above the treetops—Angelie told us we'd be indoors and enclosed—but it looks like a faraway sky. Still, that's not what keeps catching my eyes and making me blink. It's the color. I look toward where the tree trunks and branches are a sweep of gentle violets and blues. Lanterns planted among the trees cast out turquoise tendrils of light. I look away and when I turn back, the trees are back to their normal hue. All those colors—the hypnotic purples and metallic blues—have fallen to the ground as heavily as leaves. Everything looks so much brighter than I'm used to. And there's something else I can't quite define: the tiniest nearly imperceptible lag each time I look at something new.

As I take it all in, I realize that I'm not cold, and I'm not wet, and I'm not at this moment caught in a stinking, rusting, metal-edged salvage yard that's on fire. The air, so cold before, is soft and warm around me. Right now, just for now, I'm surprised to feel a small spill of something like curiosity.

In the next second, the quiet is fractured into dust. I whirl around, pivoting on my stronger leg, to see Joy with her back to Jaxon and me. She's kicking at the door we came through—the glass one that's now as opaque as concrete—and, by the look of it, trying to hack it into shards. There's some sort of fury that's boiling in her gut, that's obvious. What's weird is that she's not screaming or crying or uttering a single sound. Her kicks and hits are methodical and solid. If the door can be broken, she will do it.

But it doesn't budge. Of course. There's no going back for us. I could have told her that.

About fifty kicks past what makes sense, Joy finally stops. She turns around and strides around Jaxon and me. She doesn't look like someone who has failed, just like someone who has chosen another course. Jaxon and I watch, silent, as she jumps lightly off the end of the platform onto a narrow, slatted walkway and crosses the marsh. She's halfway up the opposite bank when Jaxon takes his own leap onto the walkway and heads after her.

I peer over the edge of the platform. It's a foot-high drop. Too much to handle on only one sure leg. I growl low in my throat, like Dublin when he's mad. We haven't even begun and my very first step is an obstacle. With one hand holding Dublin's fur in a vise grip, I hop down onto the walkway, landing on my right foot. I wobble back and forth, probably looking as shaky as the reeds, but Dublin holds firm as my anchor.

I glance ahead. Jaxon has stopped to watch me. Joy is further ahead, near the tree line, but looking back at me over her shoulder.

"We're supposed to stay together," I shout at them. "Number-one-and-only rule, remember?"

Joy shouts back at me. "I don't even know you. I don't need to. I can find the way on my own."

Fine with me, I think. *I don't need you either.* The words sound childish in my head, but I mean them. I don't know why Angelie put us all in a team. Does she think I need their help to get through this? I hate that she might believe that. I've got Dublin. He's my team. So why should I have to stay together with Joy and Jaxon? To keep us in the same time perception, I know. But Joy doesn't look like she wants to share any perceptions with anybody.

Okay, then, let her go.

I wave Joy on with a dismissive flick, but she's already heading toward the trees again.

Jaxon sprints after her and grabs her arm right before she disappears into the thick woods. He leans in close to her. Whatever he's saying is urgent but quiet. I can't hear a word. Dublin clunks onto the walkway next to me and together we navigate to the other side of the marsh. I make it up the bank just as Jaxon and Joy shift apart.

I figure they're talking about me and how I'll slow them down, so I'm surprised when Jaxon turns to me and says, "We have to stick together."

I don't want either of them doing this out of pity for me. But Jaxon gives me a half smile and shakes his head. It occurs to me that he knows exactly what I'm thinking. "Singer—that's your name, right?"

I nod.

"It's cool," Jaxon says. "There's an Irish name, Easnadh, that means musical sound."

I'm not sure what reaction he expects, so I just nod again.

He points to Joy, who is glaring at me. "Sometimes I call this one Bronagh. It means sorrow." He grins and I can't help smiling back.

"What about you?" I ask.

"Jaxon's not an Irish name, far as I know. But my dad used to call me Breacán sometimes." He points to his face and raises his eyebrows. "Freckled. Get it?"

I laugh. The noise seems out of place. "So...about sticking together?"

"Either of you have any idea what's going on? Or which way to go?" he asks. I shrug and Joy gives an edgy sigh. "Exactly. One thing I know for sure: ideas get better when more minds are working on them. So at least until we figure some of this stuff out, maybe...it makes sense to start this together?"

I don't really have a problem with that. "Like I said, we might as well follow the number-one rule. We don't know for sure what will happen if we break it."

I figure Joy will balk. Instead, she folds, though not gracefully. "I guess," she says. "For now."

Jaxon's shoulders drop, and I realize how much tension he's been holding. He doesn't want conflict, that's evident.

Jaxon puts one hand on my right arm and the other on Joy's left arm and points us both toward the woods. "Good. Because I think I *might* have an idea how to start."

He waves toward the trees. "See that? The arrow on the pine tree."

I'm not a nature girl, but I do know a pine from a palm. Those trees are not pines. They have tall trunks and lots of swoopy branches, but they must be hybrids of some sort: instead of pine needles, the branches are covered with leaves that are heart-shaped near the ground and are narrow with ragged edges higher up. "I see a *lot* of trees," I tell Jaxon. "But they don't look like pines. And I don't see any arrow."

"What are you blatherin' about?" Jaxon snorts. "Look. Carved into the trunk. You see it?"

"All I see is you having hallucinations," Joy snaps. "There's no arrow, and there's no stupid pine tree."

"Seriously? It's right *there*. Come on, I'll show you." Jaxon shakes his head at both of us and plunges into the woods, with Joy and me close behind. Once we're among the trees, they don't seem as tightly clustered. We're on a slim trail that hooks and dodges around patches of underbrush. As I concentrate on keeping up and avoiding branches that snap back from Joy's passing, I realize that Jaxon is a genius. By pretending to spot something and convincing us to follow, he's gotten all of us moving forward—together.

We walk farther than Jaxon could possibly have seen. I'm about to say something when he stops, spreads his arms wide and steps off the trail so we can see past him. "There. What did I say? An arrow."

He's not wrong.

Up close, I see it: three skinny lines joined together at one point. Yup, it's an arrow. It's etched onto a stretch of tree trunk—yes, a pine tree trunk—where the bark has been peeled off. It's pointing up, the way arrows are positioned when you're supposed to go straight ahead.

"Good spot, Eagle Scout," I say to Jaxon. "How did you even see this?"

"How did you *not*?"

Joy ignores both of us. She hovers in front of the arrow, looking left and right like she's trying to decide which way to go. My banter with Jaxon is making her impatient, I think. She seems like more of an action kind of girl. Her body reminds me of a box that's so overfilled that the lid will never completely seal shut. If you push on one side, the other snaps up. I make a mental note not to be the one who pushes.

"So. We could follow the arrow. It's here to help us, I guess. Or maybe it's part of the game to confuse us?" Jaxon paces in front of Joy. "What do you think?"

The question is meant for Joy. Nobody has asked for my opinion. Not that I have one. I'm fairly sure my decisions up to this point haven't been great ones.

Joy strides ahead. Jaxon looks back at me and shrugs, and we both follow.

I don't get far.

Dublin leaps from my side into my path. He looks up at me with his head and his bark low in a way I've never seen or heard from him before.

Then he comes at me.

He lunges again and again with his mouth gaping wide. I scream his name and reel back. He matches me step for step, swiping at me as I retreat. My heel catches on a root or stone—I don't know what—and down I go, flat on my back.

With one more leap Dublin is on top of me and at that very moment a branch cracks loose from somewhere far above us and slams down, spewing bark and caving a mark in the forest floor as it lands exactly where I stood seconds ago.

Dublin dives toward my face but he doesn't bite: he licks my nose. I lie motionless, my mind in aftershock, as his tail wags and he gives his body a shake—just like people dust off their hands after a job well done.

"Dublin, you are wild," I say. I twine my fingers into the baby-duck feather-soft fur behind his ears. "And by wild I mean you are perfect."

Joy and Jaxon have jumped over the branch—which I see, now, is as big around as a car tire—and stand in front of me with wide eyes that say it all: they didn't expect to find me alive, much less unbitten and unbroken.

"That was brutal," Jaxon says in a voice that's as shaky as my legs. "Thought you were banjaxed."

Joy glances at Dublin, then at me, then back at Dublin. "He cared more about saving you than saving himself." She lets out a long breath. "No one has ever, *ever*, done that for me."

Jaxon's face goes paler. As I get myself off the ground, he looks like he's ready to fall. There is something going on between these two. It doesn't take much insight to see that. I don't know what hidden meaning Jaxon is finding in Joy's words, but one thing I do know: the branch she just dropped on him didn't miss.

Chapter 14
Singer

This time, when we move on again, Jaxon pushes me gently into the lead.

"So you can set the pace," he explains. So—not because he or Joy have any faith in my ability to guide us across the TimeTilter.

With Dublin glued back to my side, I follow what might be a trail or might be my imagination. It's faint and zig-zaggy but there does seem to be a bit of a depression in the forest soil and a somewhat thinner layer of leaves. A path created by the game designers to lead us—or, as Jaxon suggested, to lead us astray? A voice in the back of my brain has another thought: maybe it's the trail of gamers who have passed this way. Angelie never told us whether or not we'd be alone in here. But if there was another team, they'd be on another time perception—so we'd never know anyway. Unless we bumped right into them. I'm not sure how I feel about that idea. It seems crowded enough having Joy and Jaxon with me.

Either way, the hint of a trail is all we need to keep moving.

Jaxon walks behind me and Joy follows, lagging a bit. I glance back at Jaxon's face. "Your eyes look red. Joy's too. I was just wondering...what happened?"

"That's funny." Jaxon allows himself a dim smile. "I was going to ask you the same thing."

"Fire," I say. "I was in a car..." My voice loses steam. I'm not sure how to explain to Jaxon why I was sleeping in a salvage yard.

"Sounds tough." Jaxon's smile brightens a bit. "But I can beat it. Joy and I were in a house that collapsed. It fell right on top of—" He stops himself, looks briefly over his shoulder at Joy and lowers his voice. "It fell on top of Joy. Angelie helped me pull her out."

"She—Angelie, I mean—got me away from the fire, too," I say. "She said something that kind of freaked me out. She said I was the one she'd been looking for."

"That *is* totally freaky. Like I said, I don't trust her," Joy pipes in. I guess we weren't talking as quietly as we thought. "I'm sure I saw her drive by the house a few days before it blew to pieces. I think she had something to do with that explosion."

Jaxon pauses for a moment, letting Joy catch up to him, so they're walking next to each other whether she likes it or not. "The timing is strange, I'll give you that. She was in the right place at the right time for all three of us," he says. "Still...okay...I'm a little hazy on this. I think the superzeit-whatever-thing is messing with my memory. But right before we inhaled that stuff...didn't she say that someone wants us to stay in here? And that we should be trying to get out?"

Joy flips her hand. "Of *course* we should be trying to get out. Whether she gave us some idiotic pep talk or not. She's still the one who brought us here."

"There's one thing I don't get." Jaxon hesitates. "If she wanted to put us in the TimeTilter, why would she try to burn Singer and crush us first?"

"Fair point," I say. It's true; nearly killing us before rescuing us doesn't make much sense. And Jaxon's question has sparked another one in my head. "Why did she choose *us* to be her TimeTilter team in the first place?"

Joy has a neat and fearless way with words. "Is there anyone outside this place," she asks, "who will be missing you?"

I don't have to think about that too long. My parents are away for a few days, but they'll be too busy to check on me—and they don't expect me to call them. I don't have a best friend who will be looking out obsessively for my next text. Much as it stings to admit, no one will notice if I'm not around. I let my mind loose for a minute, imagining a scene where my parents have filed a missing person report and a detective comes to the house looking for clues. Outside of my room, there's no sign that I even live there. There's no picture my parents can hand to the detective for the missing person poster.

I lay my hand on Dublin's back and turn to Jaxon. "No. There's no one to miss me."

What about Jaxon and Joy? It sounds like they were on their own. Were they homeless? I can't think of a way to ask that, especially since Joy has fallen behind again with her face blank and her eyes staring past us. She's not liking this conversation and the course it's taking.

Jaxon merely nods. "Same here."

He jiggles both arms in a shake-it-off motion, like I've seen Dublin do when he's wet. "Enough o' that. Who cares, anyway? We'll find our way out of here and get back to our sad little lives." He's smiling wide again. "In the meantime, would you *look* at this place?"

I've been so deep in our discussion that I haven't even been paying attention to the fact that we're here, completely immersed in the world of the TimeTilter. As we keep heading down the almost-trail, I take a careful look around me. It's not just time that's tilted around here, apparently. Whoever built this place had a sense of strange. I notice again that the trees look like hybrids or grafts or whatever the right word is. In this stretch of forest, I see more trees that do actually look like pines, but their needles mingle with broad oaky leaves on the same branches. The trunks arch and loop, change thickness and even share twigs and bark with their neighbors. I see long sweeps of moss around exposed roots. The same patch of moss changes color as I pass, from clover green to butter yellow to a bright turquoise that I once saw in a picture of a peacock's tail. Everything is close to familiar, but somehow shiny and off-kilter. My sight has little disconnected gaps each time I turn my head. Even the ground seems not quite reliable. With every step, I feel like my foot might not land where I expect.

I know we're in a building that has walls—somewhere—and a ceiling. But when I look up, the sky seems impossibly far away. Like miles away. Every once in a while—after stretches of time that I can't quite measure—a light mist puffs from the sky, dissipating before it reaches the treetops. I look down at the ground and don't see any shadows there. I wonder where all the daylight is coming from?

Behind me, Jaxon trips—over one of those exposed roots, I think.

"Getting tired, I guess," he says. "How long do you think we've been in here?"

I think fuzzily about what's happened since we entered. "A couple of hours?"

"So that's...what? Ten, fifteen minutes on the outside?" Jaxon sounds like he doesn't believe it.

This is hard to wrap my head around. I definitely feel—perceive—that at least a couple of hours have gone by. Yet Angelie, in real time, left us alone and closed the door on us just a handful of minutes ago? I try to concentrate, but my superzeitgebered brain is not happy to cooperate. Okay, focus. We entered the TimeTilter. Joy rushed ahead. Jaxon chased her. How did Dublin and I catch up? Not sure. But we all argued about something. Jaxon saw the arrow and we walked to it. What else? Whatever it was, it makes my stomach clench. Oh, yeah, the branch that fell. Dublin pushed me to safety.

Could all that have happened in fifteen minutes? Maybe. But it seems like we've traveled so far. I think back to the ground we've covered. Miles, surely? The terrain has gone through several miles' worth of change, I'm certain.

I sigh and keep walking. The moss has changed color again. Along this section of trail, it's blue—but not a single blue. If you named every blue thing you could think of—sky, blueberries, lake water, birthday balloons, a totaled 2003 Chevy Cobalt in a salvage yard—every shade would be matched somewhere in the moss. It's spellbinding.

Behind me, Jaxon grunts. I look back and watch him reach both arms into the empty air ahead of him like he's trying to touch something. He totters but quickly gets his feet back under him.

"You okay?" I ask.

Jaxon blinks, as if he's not quite sure, but then waves me off.

A short while later, it happens again: another stumble. The path looks smooth to me—nothing to trip over.

"Jaxon, *what* are you doing?" Joy has noticed too.

We stop and circle Jaxon.

"That was...confusing," he says. "It was like I was behind myself, watching myself."

Joy and I share a glance.

"I know. I spaced out or something. I was just going along, and I look up, and the person walking ahead of me is *me*." Jaxon talks slowly, trying to get the words out in a way that makes sense. "Singer, you were still there, up ahead. But I could see *me* walking along between us."

Jaxon sounds panicked, but Joy shrugs. "Don't go doubling yourself. One Jaxon is already too much work."

I can't laugh this off. Jaxon looks shaken. For the second time, he's seeing things that nobody else can see: first that little arrow, now a double of himself. From everything I understood before we entered the TimeTilter, the superzeitgeber is supposed to alter our perception of time. Is it doing something more to Jaxon? Altering some other perception in ways it's not supposed to? That's a thought I wish I could stash under a heavy rock and walk away from. I won't mention it to Jaxon. Not yet, anyway.

"It's okay. You're probably worn out, like you said." I give Jaxon a confident nod. He's been kind to me, and there's a comforting brightness in his wide smile. I don't want to see that light burn out so early in the game. "Let's just keep going."

I start traveling down the path again. Up to now, I've never been completely sure that I'm staying on the same trail, or if it even is a trail. There have been a few times when the shallow depressions on the forest floor have forked or faded, and I haven't seen any more arrows. Jaxon hasn't spotted any either. So where to go next has simply been a guess. My guess, since I've been in the lead.

But now the moss and the trees are drawing back and the trail is wider, so we don't need to go single file. Jaxon and Joy come up beside me. Dublin positions himself between Jaxon and me. He swipes Jaxon's hand a few times with his rough charcoal nose. He's ready to prop Jaxon up if he loses his balance again.

In another thirty minutes or so—TimeTilter minutes, anyway— we're out of the forest. I pause to rest my leg, breathe deep and take in the transitioning landscape.

I'd have appreciated a wider view of what's ahead. But that doesn't happen. Our way is blocked by a long stretch of fencing. It's made of bamboo poles that have been twined tightly together. I've never seen bamboo live and face-to-face, so I don't know if these hues ever happen in nature, but it's stunning: the smudged horizontal bands of orange and gold look like a sunset on a distant horizon. I get a vivid mental flash of the last fence I encountered: the mean chain link around the salvage yard. My palm still stings where I gashed it. But getting past this bamboo fence won't be a problem. No need to climb over or cut through it. This fence has a gate. And the gate is wide open, inviting us in.

One by one we pass through the opening. The sight on the other side doesn't exactly make my heart sing. We've left all trees behind, but this landscape will be more difficult to navigate: it's a broad swamp that's glutted with tall plumy reeds. They're so tall that I can't see over them and so thick that I don't have any sense of where the opposite edge might be. The reeds sway together, as perfectly choreographed as a swooping flock of birds.

I glance at Joy and Jaxon to see what they want to do. But Dublin makes up his own mind. He noses forward into the swamp, tail wagging like it does when he sees a new person he wants to meet.

I grab his collar as he shoulders his way in. I look back just as the reeds start to close up behind me and grab Jaxon's hand. I don't want us to lose sight of each other now. Jaxon pulls Joy in with him and that's how we go forward, awkwardly linked together.

I don't notice what's missing right away.

I duck my head and focus myopically on each next step. The ground is mucky and sucks at my shoes. I sink and pull loose and watch my sneakers get soaked and splattered. The reeds keep brushing against me and tangling around my legs.

Then I get it. What's missing is sound.

All of this is happening in complete...and total...silence.

Chapter 15
Singer

I should hear the squelch of mud and the scratch of the reeds. I should hear Dublin panting and Joy making a sarcastic comment.

But I don't. Not a single sound.

I pull Dublin to a stop and whip around. Joy and Jaxon are both staring at me with wide eyes. So they've noticed it too.

What they don't notice is the shape weaving through the reeds behind them and coming directly toward Joy.

It's no more than a swish. A shred of black shadow.

Whatever it is, when it reaches Joy it does the impossible.

It merges right into her.

I watch Joy's lips part in what might be a breath or might be a scream but I'll never know because sound has forsaken us. We are left silent and alone as Joy's body turns into a stark silhouette that jitters and sparks.

Jaxon never lets go. He keeps Joy's hand tight in his own.

Which means it's his turn next.

The shadow slides from Joy to Jaxon through their linked hands. Joy, released, begins to sink to the ground. Jaxon, his face tight with pain, makes an agonized turn toward me and lets me go.

His lips move and I think he says, *"Run!"*

The seconds surge by but I can't move. I won't. The shadow sweeps through Jaxon and leaves him and I should be next but Jaxon has broken the chain. This is my chance.

I reach out for Jaxon's hand and clutch it tight. With my other hand I give Dublin's collar a shake and he knows, somehow he knows, exactly what I want him to do.

Dublin takes off with a leap that in my other normal world of another time I could never match, but he has enough strength for both of us. We run through the swamp as if the ground were not muck and the reeds were not thick as nightmares. We reach another bamboo fence and Dublin and I smash against it together, shoulder to shoulder.

The bamboo poles bend and bow.

We break through. Dublin and I, then Jaxon, then Joy.

The bamboo snaps upright behind us and the shadow is gone.

In an instant we are reunited with sound.

Jaxon bends over Joy, saying something in her ear. Dublin sticks his muzzle up against my cheek and huffs. Usually when he does that I push him away, but this time I want him close. The noise of Dublin's snuffling breath—yes, that definitely makes my heart sing.

Chapter 16
Singer

We are out and we are safe.

"What happened?" Jaxon tones down his voice as if a normal volume would be too loud after all that dead silence. "What happened back there?"

Joy is back on her feet. She looks like she doubts her own balance. "Angelie," Joy snaps. "She never warned us that there are...things... in here that would go after us."

"At least it's not following us. Maybe the fence keeps it in the swamp?" Jaxon tosses a glance at the fence, which certainly didn't keep us from busting through. Then he turns to me. "You should have run when I told you to. But...I'm glad you didn't."

I nod, grateful for the acknowledgement, but that's the end of my participation in this conversation. My breaths are still coming too fast. I stand bent over, hands on my knees, chest sucking in air. My mouth is as dry as a summer of drought. I am so intensely thirsty that I could cry—though there's no moisture in my body to spare for tears. Worst of all, the grinding in my leg is growing stronger.

I'm used to a spike in the pain when I walk too much, move too much, and—like now—when I'm dehydrated and beyond stressed. But this is past anything I'm used to dealing with. I had medication for the pain. There were a few more pills in the little orange bottle from the pharmacy that I left behind on my nightstand. But that's no help to me now.

You just need water, my tired mind insists. Cold, delicious, wet water. Streaming from a silver faucet. Dancing with ice cubes in a tall glass. Rushing, raining, soothing water...yeah, I am definitely dehydrated.

"Singer! Over here!" Jaxon shouts.

I rise, every inch an effort. Jaxon and Joy have walked ahead while I was resting. They're standing next to each other and staring down. Whatever they're looking at, it's rejuvenating them in a way that makes my dry, tired body prickle. I hobble toward them. When I reach Joy's side, I start to take another step forward—just to prove I can move on with them. Joy sucks in a breath and grabs my arms and pulls me back and in that second, looking down, I realize that if she had let me go I would have fallen nearly two hundred feet to my death.

"What...is that?" I say tentatively.

"It's a pit for holding idiots," Joy says roughly. "Look where you're going next time."

I'm too busy trying to process what just happened to deal with Joy's attitude. I take three steps back. From here, what I'm sure I see is a wide stretch of grass—lush and clipped as a freshly mown field—spreading from our feet to another tree line in the distance. I move back next to Joy and Jaxon. The field disappears as neatly as if it never existed, and, peering down again, I see that we're standing on one rim of a deep gorge. The field is an optical illusion—another offbeat note in the landscape.

What if I really had walked over the edge? Surely there would be a safety net somewhere down there to catch me? After all, being in the TimeTilter is supposed to be an adventure. A game. Not a deathtrap. Still, I don't have any interest in putting that to the test.

Of bigger interest to me is what's at the bottom of the gorge. A river. A bubbling, swirling, rushing, singing river. It's beautiful.

It's water.

I need to get down there.

With my toes inches away from the rim, I peer down. The cliff is the kind of steep that makes my legs start a shiver that runs up my spine. The face of the cliff is all points and ledges of rock that cave in and spike out in shades of glistening grey. A couple of courageous trees are trying to make a go of it in scant patches of soil. The drop is so vertical that the tree trunks are growing parallel to the cliff side.

The cliff doesn't look navigable by Joy and Jaxon, much less me.

The gorge, viewed from the rim, goes on left and right as far as I can see—a decisive break, like an unbreachable castle moat, stopping our forward progress.

But at the bottom, down a couple hundred feet that might as well be miles, is my motivation. The sweet river. Ripples, wakes, and small isles of fresh white foam mark the water's easy flow. The river swings in lazy S-curves. The riverbed looks wide and deep, though it's tough to be sure of dimensions from up here.

"Any ideas for getting down there?" I ask.

"I don't care about down, just across," Jaxon says.

I'm ready to let loose a few slashing words, because doesn't he understand that nothing is more important to me right now than that water? But when Jaxon gives me another of his light smiles, I remember. He and Joy don't have any idea how thirsty and tired

I am. I swallow back my anger. They're already slowing down for me. I don't want them to feel like they have to make any more concessions.

"Why even bother with across?" Joy says. She glances at my leg. "That's not happening. Let's just go right or left and see where it gets us. It'll make as much random sense as anything else we've done."

"This is starting to spook me." Jaxon shakes his head. "Am I really the only one seeing this?" He gazes across the gorge.

"An arrow? You see one again?" Joy's voice wavers between disbelief and relief. I know she'd prefer an action plan.

"It's true. I swear." Jaxon points at the opposite rim. "Right there."

Joy tilts her head as she looks across the void. "Okay. I think I see it too."

Jaxon laughs. "Yeah, sure you do. You're looking the wrong way." He holds Joy's shoulders and points her slightly to the right.

For the first time, Joy looks flustered. She jerks loose from Jaxon's grip and edges away from us. Jaxon's forehead wrinkles. I think now he's sorry he teased her. He goes after her, while I stand stock still at the rim and gaze down at the river.

"How are we supposed to get over there?" Jaxon says. His head is bent close to Joy and his back is to me, but I can still hear their conversation.

"And then get back up the other side?" Joy shoots back. "Even if we could make it, like I said, it's not going to happen for *her*. We've been following her for a long time and look where it's gotten us. Literally to the edge of nowhere."

I don't move, pretending I'm completely focused on watching the water and don't hear a thing, but I can see from the corner of my eye that Joy isn't even checking whether I'm in earshot. Maybe I should say something, speak up and shut her up. But I stay quiet. Part of me wants to know the truth about what she really thinks of me. And then I find out.

"She's totally a liability. You know that, Jaxon. She led us here, and now she can't climb down or up." Joy sighs. "So if we stick with her, we're stuck."

Chapter 17
Singer

It was Joy's sigh that got me.

Just like my mom's. So much expressed in a simple outward breath. Some anger. Some impatience. Mostly "doneness." As in, "I'm so done with Singer." I know my mom felt burdened with me, the problem baby who ate up health insurance co-payments with every visit to the hospital and made her miss one competition after another trying to get to all the doctor appointments that fixed nothing. She got tired of that, eventually. Tired of me. And weariness led to resentment. I tried to keep that from happening with Joy and Jaxon but once again I've wholly and utterly failed.

I turn away from the two of them. If I had an ounce of moisture in my eyes I'd be crying, so dehydration seems, just this once, like something to be thankful for. My leg still throbs and now my head has joined the pain party.

With no water and no medication, I have only one source of comfort.

Dublin.

With my back to the gorge, I reach for him at my side. He's not there. With a lurch of delayed awareness, I realize he hasn't been next to me since Joy kept me from falling over the cliff.

There's no way he could have fallen over the rim without one of us seeing—so I won't give that scenario another second of attention. But there's something else, nearly as bad: perception failure. Those were the words Angelie used. If Dublin goes out of my sight for too long, he goes out of my perception. I won't be able to find him, no matter how hard I look. I will lose him.

 "Dublin!" I scream his name using every bit of breath in my lungs. "Dublin! Dublin!" I scream so loudly that his name travels across the gorge and comes back to me in a taunting playback.

And I run—my own hobbling way-too-slow version of run. Along the rim of the gorge. Down to the hedge and back in furious, helpless circles. Up to Joy and Jaxon, shaking them and begging them to help me search. All the while I know it's hopeless. I've lost sight of Dublin. I've let him stray. And that means he's lost sight of me. Is he searching for me too, circling in the same frantic patterns, barking desperately?

I can't stand the thought of it and my brain begins to fog.

I keep moving, stretching the reach of my hunt further along the gorge, and I never stop yelling his name. I weave back to the bamboo fence, staring at the place where we busted through. I know, I absolutely know, that Dublin came out with me. And I know, I absolutely know, that I don't want to go back that way. Still...it's the one place I haven't searched.

I reach one hand toward the fence. And then two things happen at once.

Jaxon—he must have been following me, sensing what I was thinking—grabs my wrist with a rattled "Stop!"

And Joy, at the same moment, says in a voice that's loud but infuriatingly calm: "Look. There he is."

I swing around, Jaxon's hand still on my wrist like he's afraid of what I'll do next. Joy points over her shoulder and there my dog stands, as if he was waiting in that spot the entire time. He's fine, he's okay—that's the first thing I see. His head is high and his tail is doing its happy pendulum sweep. I shake Jaxon loose and cover the distance to Dublin in one beat of my heart.

The hug I hold him in is long and fierce. After I sit back, I see he's covered in loose dirt and a few sticky smears of cobweb. I run my hands over him, nose to toes to tail, over and over, as much to clean him up as to feel the silky solid here-ness of him.

"Where was he?" Jaxon asks the question that's bumping around in my head.

"I have no idea. He was *gone*. And suddenly we can see him again?" I shrug. "I guess...the whole perception failure thing doesn't apply to dogs?"

From my ground-level view of Dublin, I get a good look at his paws. "His claws are a mess. Packed with dirt." I lift one paw up for Jaxon and Joy to see. "Wherever he was, he's been digging."

"Digging?" Joy sounds surprised. "Where?" There's a long pause while she watches Dublin. Then, without another word, Joy pushes past us. She starts kicking at mounds of rocks and stamping down messy crosshatches of weeds.

When she doesn't find whatever it is she's looking for, Joy spreads her arms wide and crouches down by Dublin. "Okay, dog. Where was it? Where were you digging?"

Now it's my turn to be surprised—because Dublin, in his own way, answers. He pops up with his mouth gaping in what looks exactly like a grin. Then he brushes by Joy and trots off without looking back.

Jaxon grabs my hand and hoists me to my feet. We follow Joy, who's following Dublin. In single file we all make our way along the edge of the gorge.

Dublin stops in front of a high tangle of red vines that's well past where I searched for him. Joy doesn't hesitate. She reaches in with both hands and parts the vines and cobwebs. When she turns back to us, she turns up her lips in the very first smile I've seen on her face and says, "There."

Sure enough, she's found something. Jaxon and I crowd in around Joy to see. At first I think it's just a hole in the ground. Its outer edges are raked and gouged from Dublin's claws. What was he after? When I look further in, I can see the bottom of the hole. Something about it looks odd. Like it's not dirt, but wood and bits of metal. Then I get it: beneath the vines and dirt that Dublin has scraped away is, in fact, a door.

A trapdoor.

The door is made of scarred and pocked oak wood that looks hundreds of years old. It's the kind of door I've seen in photos of historic, cobble-stoned side alleys in quaint Italian villages.

In one fluid motion Joy drops, grabs hold of an iron ring in the center of the wooden slats and pulls with all her might. Someone must be keeping the hinges in great shape: the door swings open with no resistance at all.

With two feet already sliding down past the open entry, Joy looks up at me. "There's a staircase. I guess you'll get to your river after all."

I watch Joy and Jaxon pass through the opening and begin their descent. Beneath my hand, Dublin shifts. His dark round eyes meet mine. I know what he's asking: do we follow?

I am as dried out as desert sand, my leg is hurting without mercy and my equilibrium is barely held in place. But there is nowhere else to go but down.

I nod to Dublin and point to the stairs. Yes. We follow.

It's a spiral staircase, and each step is a short drop to the next one. I can navigate them with a tight grip on the handrail, so Dublin gets a break from steadying me. Still, it's a long way down. I rest when I can. Joy and Jaxon adjust their pace so that I can keep them in sight. For a while our path is lit from the entryway above. When that brightness fades, our footfalls activate rings of motion-activated lights. Because we're underground, I expected dirt walls, but the surfaces are sleek, grey and seamless. The air is cold in here. It feels like the inside of a freezer. I watch my breath puff out in front of me in small clouds—a welcome reminder that my lungs are still working, even if the rest of me feels like a salvage yard heap.

Down.

And down.

Joy and Jaxon, ahead of me on the staircase, drop lower and lower. I put more of my weight on the handrail and let my feet slide from step to step. It's a bit faster but my arms start to burn.

Just when I'm sure I'll scream if there's one more turn of the spiral, I see it: a very literal light at the end of the tunnel. There's no door, just an arched opening in the wall. Jaxon waits for me at the bottom step. He takes my arm without saying anything, but he must have noticed that my breathing is raspy and I'm having trouble keeping upright. Joy looks back and with a brief frown takes my other arm. Linked together, we walk out into the bottom of the gorge.

I try to look up the sheer sides of the cliff. It must be beautiful, a sheer rocky rise on either side of us, but I don't even have the energy to lift my head. It feels like the sun has a vendetta against me and has decided to slam every ray it has at me. It's that hot. Then I remember there is no sun. I give another internal nod to the designer of this place for making the environment so believably real—but in the next second I don't care.

Joy and Jaxon are half carrying and half dragging me forward and now that I see where we're heading, I give them all the help I can.

The river. From this angle, the flow looks faster than it did from above. Water droplets pop and swirl around rock tips that rise up from the dark riverbed. But it's not that deep. I can see the bottom. When we reach the bank and Joy and Jaxon let go of me, I just keep going. I forge ahead, down the bank and deep into the water and then I'm down on my knees, bending over and plunging my face into the river.

As soon as my skin hits the surface, I lose all rational thought. I am an animal, acting on instinct, downing the water in greedy gulps as if I could drink the river dry. I drink and drink until it feels like every one of my cells is saturated. Only when my stomach is filled and rounded do I finally stop. Then I sink deeper into the water, closing my eyes against the bright light that looks like a sun.

The current flirts with me, lapping against my body and tugging me gently downstream. I keep a light hold onto the riverbed so that I don't get swept away.

From upstream come the sounds of Jaxon and Joy splashing in the water. There's a bark of actual laughter from Jaxon that sounds so disjointed down here in the quiet bottom of the gorge that I want to shush him. But when I raise my head, I see Jaxon sloshing in circles around Joy and they're both smiling, and it's a small moment between them that I don't want to shatter.

I get to my feet. Dublin, belly-deep in the water, shakes himself right next to me and now I'm laughing too.

I peer down at him, all drenched and sleek. His feathery fur floats and fans out into the water like mermaid hair and it's the most beautiful thing I've ever seen.

I reach out to touch him and he begins to swirl, spinning around and around until he blurs. Then the weirdest thing happens: the river pulls back, like it's giving him a moment to shine, giving him room to dance. Dublin billows out, filling the space like fire. Slowly the water slides back in, rising around us in a glinting silver-satin wave. I step toward the wave and slide inside it, but in a shutter-blink I am jolted back to where I started. My stomach spasms. Dublin spins, but his eyes hold mine and never move, never waver.

In the back of my mind I understand that none of this makes sense.

I tilt my head back and gaze up at the sun that isn't a sun. The wave glides in and warps around me and I rise high high high above the river to the top of the gorge. *I'm letting you go now*, the wave tells me. I look down the sheer side of the cliff where intervals of time jut out in ragged slices and I know that on the way down my body will hit every one.

Chapter 18
Jaxon

"Look at her." Joy's voice was so hard and cold it sounded like ice cubes hitting glass.

Joy had waded across the river to the far bank and Jaxon had followed, stomping in the water with each step just for the fun of seeing how high he could send up a splash. Now, done abruptly with playing, he pulled up and wheeled toward her. "What?"

"Look." Joy jerked her chin.

Jaxon, still ankle-deep in the cooling flow, swiveled around to look back to where they'd started. Singer was still there. He had watched her drink so desperately and deeply that he had thought she might burst. She was upright now but turning slowly in place with her head down, like she was looking for something below the surface of the river.

"She's tired," Jaxon said.

"She's acting strange. Watch."

Jaxon focused on Singer. There *was* the look of a weird water creature about her, no doubt of that. Her wet hair hung sleek against her head and draped over her shoulders. Her arms were limp at her sides. From this distance it was hard to be certain, but her eyes looked closed. With each revolution in the water, Singer rocked forward slightly and then snapped upright.

"What's she doing?" Jaxon kept his voice low, though there was no real chance of Singer hearing him.

"She's freaking me out."

Jaxon gave Joy a glance. He knew that look on her face. She wasn't joking and she wasn't being cruel. Joy was truly unnerved.

"Hey." Jaxon stepped toward her. "What's going on?"

Joy arched her shoulders and sighed. "I hate this place, Jax. Why would any gamer pay to get in here? It's horrible. We need to get out of here. We're not moving fast enough. Forget Singer. Look at *me*." She thrust one arm toward Jaxon with her hand splayed flat. Her long slim fingers trembled.

Jaxon caught her hand in his own and gently squeezed her fingers still. "I know it, Bronagh. It's a rough place. We're all worn out."

Joy shook her head. "No, it's more than that. Everything feels so *wrong* in here. I'm not just tired. I'm wiped out. My muscles feel like they're going to fail. I need to get out, Jax. We need to move faster and get to the end." Joy looked past him at Singer. "We need to cut her loose."

Jaxon checked Singer's progress across the river. She hadn't moved forward at all. As he watched, her head drooped further. "What are you saying? We can't leave her. You know that."

"I *can* leave her. I will." Joy swallowed. "I'm going to keep moving. I'm going to get out of here." She pulled her hand loose from Jaxon. "I'm asking you this time, Jax. Come with me."

Joy, his own Joy, wanting him with her. The words thrummed in his head, blurring his vision.

Ever since the explosion—no, well before that—he had felt her slipping away. Keeping up with her made him feel like a tracker in the woods, looking for footprints and cracked branches and other signs of her passing that were becoming less and less distinct. Allowing Angelie to bring them both here was not his only mistake, but in Joy's eyes it was his worst. He should have found another way. He should have busted open the back of Angelie's grey van, gathered Joy to his side and jumped. Where they landed wouldn't have mattered to Joy because she would be free. Instead, Jaxon had let this happen, had ignored her pleas and her panic, and now here they were, trapped like a pacing pack of wolves in the zoo. They would be stronger and much faster without Singer. If Jaxon, right now, turned his back on Singer, took Joy's hand back and ran— surely it would align them again. And Joy would finally understand how little anything else in the world mattered to him.

"You have to make a choice," Joy said. She was out of the water. She backed away from the river, one shuffling step at a time, her blue-soled running shoes scraping across the rocks. She wanted him to follow.

He had to follow.

Don't look. Don't look back. The words thudded in Jaxon's head, loud as a bullhorn.

And yet he looked back, his eyes ripping across the river, not wanting to see.

Dead ahead, Singer wobbled briefly, arms outstretched, and then fell face-forward into the water. The river curled around her, gathered her into its liquid arms and began to float her gently downstream.

The water. The river. Singer drinking, drinking, until she nearly choked. Just like Joy said, something had felt so wrong—somehow Jaxon had known it all along and now it jumped into cutting clarity: the water. Singer had drunk the water. He and Joy had not.

Behind Jaxon, Joy's back was turned to him. She trudged toward the far wall of the gorge.

"Joy!" Jaxon yelled, but she didn't hear him, or wouldn't hear him. Jaxon yelled again, an incoherent roar that charged up the cliff and pelted back down. He had no choice. This. Was. Not. A. Choice. How could he even have considered abandoning Singer, when he knew so well what it felt like to be left behind?

Jaxon plunged down the river, his desperate steps smashing the water's surface and sending up a jagged spray. When he reached Singer, he pulled her upright and to his amazement she not only stood but fought him with all her might, slinging at him with random fists and gushing words that made no sense.

Next to Singer, Dublin eyed Jaxon fiercely and let out a steady beat of throaty barks.

"Back down. I won't hurt her." Jaxon aimed the words at Dublin as if the dog could understand.

Jaxon grabbed Singer's flailing arms and dragged her toward the opposite bank. The water—which at first had felt so cooling and soothing—now snapped icily at his ankles. Singer kicked at him and her sneaker flew off, arching high and then plunging toe-first back into the river far upstream. Her other foot, taking its own turn at a kick, was shoeless too. Jaxon dodged a head-butt and wrapped his arms tightly around Singer, lifting her up until her feet were above the water. Just a few more yards and they were out of the river.

Jaxon set Singer down. All the fight had washed out of her. She stood eerily still, staring downward with eyes as hard as river stone. Jaxon stood too, panting and dripping, with no idea what to do next.

Joy, it seemed, wasn't having that problem. Jaxon watched her move along the base of the cliff with one hand flat against the rock wall. She hadn't rushed after Jaxon to help him with Singer, apparently hadn't even bothered to watch his frantic rescue. No, her back was turned, and she was moving away, searching for a way out of the gorge. Jaxon dropped his arms and closed his eyes. He needed this rest, this blank blackness, just for a moment. He needed a break from seeing Joy choose the way she always chose: forward and free without him, instead of struggling together, side by side.

When Jaxon opened his eyes, he saw two things with stabbing clarity. One of these things was Joy, now standing in front of a rectangular gap in the cliff wall that was partly obscured by a curtain of dangling cherry-red vines. She had found it, the way up and out of the gorge. She wasn't looking back, but she wasn't gone yet. Still, at any moment she might decide to disappear into the gap and be out of Jaxon's sight and perception.

The other thing Jaxon saw was an empty space where Singer had been only seconds before. She was winding her way back toward the water. He shouldn't have let go of her, not for an instant. Dublin bounced desperately at Singer's side, nearly tripping Singer up in an attempt to stop her. So even the dog was a better guardian than Jaxon.

Jaxon covered the space between them in seconds. He grasped at Singer's arm. Her skin, still sleek with water, slipped away. He nearly gave up at that second, gave up Joy and Singer and the will to follow one and save the other. But there, at his feet, stood Dublin. Something was bulging out of his soft mouth. Something black and sodden with two long ribbony strands trailing down. It was a sneaker. Singer's missing sneaker, the mate to the one she had kicked into the river.

"Dublin, give it!" he commanded. The dog dropped the shoe right into his open hands. Jaxon dropped to his knees and pressed his forehead to Dublin's and felt his chest choke with gratitude, because just for once something was happening without a struggle.

Then he moved, as fast as he could. With determined jerks he tugged the wet shoelace free. He caught up to Singer and rotated her away from the water, facing back to the cliff. Jaxon tied one end of the shoelace around her wrist and looped the other end in his hand. He gave a light tug and when she responded with a step his way—blind-eyed and zombie-stiff but still, a step—Jaxon's chest constricted again. Now they were connected. Now he wouldn't lose her or have to leave her behind.

The three of them—Jaxon and Singer, with Dublin in their wake—retraced their path to the face of the cliff.

Joy was still there, at the entryway to another spiral staircase that would take them to the top of the gorge. She raised her eyebrows but didn't quite meet Jaxon's gaze.

"The water..." Jaxon said softly.

"...was filled with superzeitgeber," Joy finished. "I know. That's what I think, too. That mist, it settles in the water. She got a ton of superzeitgeber in her body from drinking so much."

Jaxon nodded. So she hadn't been watching him with Singer, but she had been thinking and wondering what was going on. That was something.

"She overdosed. On time perception," Jaxon said. The words sounded foolish but Joy didn't laugh.

"Maybe it'll wear off. Either way, let's go." She looked at Jaxon once, honestly and unblinkingly, then headed toward the stairs. An apology, maybe, Jaxon thought. At least another invitation to follow.

He headed after her and started up the staircase, tugging Singer along behind him. It was a replay of their journey down into the gorge, only this time upward, moving one after the other into an unknown. With each step, Singer jerked and balked and spouted sounds that Jaxon had never heard before.

He held tight to his end of the shoelace. The fraying strand of cotton was his only hope of holding on to Singer. And it was Singer's only hope of holding on to their narrow strip of shared time.

Chapter 19
Monet

To: Director of Security
Subject: ID Card

Hello,

I've reached out to you several times about my ID card being rejected and the matter still hasn't been resolved. Please get back to me as soon as possible.

Monet Jourdain

Monet clicked the Send button with a steady finger. But inside she was a roiling mess. Three days had passed and still she couldn't access the TimeTilter building, from the North entrance or from any other. She'd moved up the chain of command, calling and emailing higher and higher levels of security. She had even left a message for Dr. Angelie Bonneville.

No one was answering.

Why was she being shut down? There was really only one possible answer. She was going to be fired. Monet Jourdain, the one-time rising star, was now falling roughly to earth.

It was the flaw in the floating ceiling. It had to be. Or maybe her design was simply too mundane. Maybe her landscape fell short of the wondrous, mind-bending vision that Dr. Bonneville had hoped for. Or was it something else entirely, something she'd forgotten or never seen? The doubts poked viciously at Monet, tangling her thoughts and twisting her stomach.

She started another email in her head, to her sister this time: *Hi. You'll never guess what happened. I got fired. My career is over. On the bright side, I'm coming home. Please tell Mom. Hey, you and I can be roomies again! Ha ha. See you soon.*

The knock at Monet's door was the last thing in the world she was expecting at that moment—and the best possible sound she could imagine. In an instant, all her doubts slid away and a whole new scenario played out in her mind: this would be someone from security who would apologize for the mix-up and hand her a shiny new ID card and together they would laugh at the company's ineptness at internal communication.

Monet jumped up from her swivel chair and ran to open the door.

The man on the other side of it was, no question about it, not from security. He was lanky and slouched and had untrimmed hair that curled around his ears. He wore a washed-out pale blue button-down shirt that hung loose over his jeans. His hazel eyes widened at the sight of her, as if he recognized her.

"Hello, I'm Hunter Slope." He extended a hand for her to shake.

"From over, um, you know, from over in the programming division? And you're Monet Jourdain, right? I mean, I know you are. I've seen you before."

This was so much awkwardness all at once that Monet moved several steps back into her office. Hunter Slope followed her in and leaned against her bookcase, nudging a whole row of books to the back of the shelf.

"You know me...how?" Monet asked, both eyebrows raised high.

"Well, you know, from your profile. Online. On the employee website. Everyone in my division read it." Hunter smiled. "You're kind of a folk hero to my group."

Monet remembered the piece. She was named Employee of the Month not long after she was hired. Someone had interviewed her and turned all her words into some graceful prose that made her sound smart and humble at the same time.

"That profile..." Monet began. "It's old news. I don't think the company likes me that much right now."

"Ahhh, a rebel?" Hunter said with a wider grin.

Monet had to smile back. "Not exactly. More like a ghost."

"Hmm, intriguing." He paused and stared at Monet. She stared right back. It was, in fact, kind of reassuring to know that someone in this company could see her and hear her.

"I guess," Hunter finally said, "I should tell you why I'm here." He straightened up for a moment before his shoulders slowly inched back down, as if good posture was simply too great a burden. "It's, um, well, it's complicated. I'm not sure where to begin."

"Maybe with that?" Monet pointed down to Hunter's right foot, where a tightly folded strip of yellow paper was slipping down past the bottom hem of his jeans.

"Oh. Yes. That would be a good start." He bent double to retrieve the paper and when he rose his face was red. "I didn't want anyone to see this. So I tucked it in my sock. Well, I thought I did. But I'm not, actually, um—this may surprise you—I'm not very good at hiding things."

Hunter gave Monet's desk a questioning pat, and when she nodded, he unfolded the paper and laid it flat. "Before I explain... would you mind, you know, closing the door? And locking it?"

Monet almost laughed. She could imagine herself trying to explain this moment to her sister, who would shriek: *You SO did not do that!* But there was something about Hunter—something real and troubled in his grey eyes. He was taking a leap by trusting her, not the other way around. And so, she did it. She walked to the door, gently closed it and pressed the lock in the doorknob.

She bent over the desk next to Hunter. The crinkled paper lay beneath his splayed hands.

Trial - Subject	Enhancement	
02-01-DM	**Chrono**	
	Description:	Visual temporal perception of past events
	Delivery:	Stimulation of medial temporal lode for hyper-replay of neural activity
	Extent:	RT 30 to RT 90 previous days
	Manifestation:	Single persona timeline
	Goals:	Intentional control
02-02-DM2	**Ultraviolet**	
	Description:	Visual perception of ultraviolet spectrum
	Delivery:	Lens implantation
	Extent:	30 PHz to 750 THz
	Manifestation:	Perception of UV wavelengths
	Goals:	Realization of full extent

02-03-RT	**Microscopic**	
	Description:	Visual perception of entities below human diffraction limit
	Delivery:	Lens implantation
	Extent:	0.001 mm to 0.02 mm
	Manifestation:	Observation of gaps lower than 0.026 mm at 15-cm distance
	Goals:	Clarity; fine tuning of focus
03-01-SS	**Night**	
	Description:	Visual perception under dark ambient conditions
	Delivery:	Implantation of reflective coating and rhodopsin-flooded retinal rods
	Extent:	64 to 72 lp/mm
	Manifestation:	High resolution in reduced illumination
	Goals:	Improved re-adaptation to regular light
03-02-JM	**Telescopic**	
	Description:	Visual perception of remote objects
	Delivery:	Implantation of second enhanced fovea centralis
	Extent:	20/5 resolution
	Manifestation:	Visual acuity at distances of two miles
	Goals:	Improved resolution
03-03-JB	**Shared**	
	Description:	Projection of perceived sight
	Delivery:	Implantation of transmitter in optic nerve
	Extent:	One recipient
	Manifestation:	Intended recipient's vision is overlaid with shared sight
	Goals:	Multiple recipients; projection of past events

"What am I looking at?"

Hunter's finger trailed down the paper. "This column. On the left. I don't know exactly what the numbers and letters stand for. But the notes on the right, I've been reading those over and over. It all seems related to...well...to vision. Different ways to enhance a person's vision."

"Enhanced vision. Okay." Monet leaned in for a closer look at the tiny text. "Chrono vision? Shared vision? Some of these sound kind of odd."

"Yes. It's, um, most definitely odd. Like something out of a superhero movie."

"So...maybe someone's designing a fantasy gaming scenario?"

"That's what I thought at first. But something else is going on. Something strange." Hunter looked sideways at Monet. He was heading somewhere with this, she was sure.

"Not to be rude," she said gently, "but can we get to the point? Why are you showing me this?"

"Yes. Well. Here's the thing." Hunter pushed up his sleeves. "The way I got this document was, um, to be honest, not actually entirely... that is to say, if people insist on having inadequate passwords, and 12345 is not an adequate password, let me tell you, well then, they shouldn't be surprised if their emails are, you know..."

Monet stepped back from the paper. "Are you telling me you *hacked* someone's email to get this information?"

Hunter met her eyes squarely. "Yes, in fact, that is what I did. And I believe I had good reason to do so. The document, well, you see, it was attached to an email, Monet. A very brief email with a message that I know, um, I know will interest you."

"What was it?"

Hunter slid the paper off the desk, flipped it over and held it flat in front of her. The text of the email, as Hunter had said, was brief:

Research going forward. Shut down all non-essential access to TT.

Monet felt a weird quiver that started in her stomach and ran all the way down to her toes.

"Hunter," she said slowly. "I've been shut out of the TimeTilter. I haven't been able to get in for days. But you already knew that, didn't you? You saw my email to the Director of Security."

Hunter's nod was barely visible. "Yes. Sorry about that. But, well, you should know...you're not the only one whose access has been blocked."

The quiver in Monet's stomach spiked upward. *Denied access.* The words zipped and flashed in her head like electrical sparks. She couldn't get past them to think. "I don't understand. Five minutes ago I thought I was being fired. What's happening here?"

"I'm beginning to put it all together," Hunter said. "But I need your help."

"*My* help." Monet shook her head. "What could I possibly do?"

"Well. As I said before, I read your, um, profile. You know every inch of the TimeTilter. You know it better than anyone else in this company. The layout. The landscape. The structure. The rules. Am I right about that?"

Hunter's words could have been taken as excessive flattery, meant to ease her into agreement. But to Monet, what he was saying was simply the truth. She had spent uncountable hours in the TimeTilter, designing and dreaming and directing. She would have slept there if that had been allowed.

"Something strange...that is to say, something *wrong* is going on in there." Hunter tapped the wrinkled paper. "I want to know, um, what that is. Don't you?"

Hunter was right. The TimeTilter was her domain. And she did, very much, want to know what was going on in there. Still...

"If you think something bad is happening, why don't you go to the police?" Monet said, lifting her chin in a final challenge.

Hunter's slouch deepened. "That, in fact, is the last thing I would do. The roots of this thing go deep. One of the emails that I, um, uncovered—or, as you said, *hacked*—well, let me say this, Monet." He fixed his eyes on hers. "I don't think there are very many people we can trust."

Chapter 20
Singer

When I wake, I'm sitting with my back propped against a tree and my face is wet.

As my senses reluctantly reboot, the first thing I see is a motionless heap of gold fur. It's Dublin. He's deep asleep.

Every cell in my body is trying to sweet-talk me into passing back out. I've never been much good at fighting sleep. With a heavy breath, I slump sideways. But halfway down, I catch sight of Jaxon and Joy with their backs to me, bent over something I can't see.

I know that I'm in the TimeTilter, but I have no idea why I'm in this exact spot or how I got here. This much I dimly understand: I have to get back in the game.

Here is how it goes: I sit upright. My head pounds. I fumble to rise, but without Dublin's help I go back down in a graceless sprawl. I try again with all the strength I have right now. Slowly... slowly...I stand. The world spins.

I breathe as deeply as I can, pulling in the cool and piney night air.

Daylight is fading quickly, but even so I can see that I'm in a clearing. It's a round space of tamped-down soil and soft leaves, ringed by fat-trunked barkless trees and spindly plants with exotic purple flowers.

At the far edge of the clearing, Joy and Jaxon are hunched over with their hands on their knees. So odd. What are they doing? I take a few steps closer and then I see. They've gathered branches and brush and they're trying to build a shelter.

Without warning, my stomach pitches like a rowboat caught in a squall. I stagger toward the trees and let it all go, coughing the contents of my gut into the bushes.

When I'm done, Jaxon is beside me with his hand on my shoulder.

"You're back," he says simply, as if I've returned from a quick walk to the market to get a soda.

Before I speak, I take stock of myself. My headache is dwindling away. I'm not thirsty anymore. That, all by itself, is a mercy.

"Do you remember anything?" Jaxon begins.

I shake my head. My memories feel like muddy storm water that has swirled into a dark city-street gutter. The last coherent image I have is seeing the river and plunging in to drink.

"It's been...kind of...you were..." he trails off.

I can't begin to imagine what happened, and that fact is making my stomach feel shaky again.

"It's better if she knows exactly what she put you through." Joy's voice carries from where she's crouched by the stockpile of sticks. She marches toward me with a spiny branch in one hand and for a quick moment I think she's coming over to hit me with it. But when Joy reaches me, her eyes are serious but not angry.

"The river was loaded with superzeitgeber," she says bluntly. "You drank a *lot* of water. So we figure you got such a big dose that it totally messed up your sense of time. I don't know what you were seeing all that time, but it wasn't anything real." She pauses, but I don't speak. Whatever I saw, it's lost now. "You nearly drowned. Jaxon pulled you out of the water and got you up out of the gorge and after that we went for—I don't know—hours, I guess. Sometimes you just walked along and sometimes you freaked out, but he got you here."

I run a hand through my hair, pushing it out of my eyes. Jaxon stands silent between Joy and me. For the first time I register that his face is raw and exhausted. Joy's wrap-up of everything that happened is, I'm sure, leaving out a lot of ugly details. I open my mouth. No sound comes out because I'm not sure what to say.

Joy isn't finished. "I just want to make sure you understand. I would have left you behind. It's not your fault, but you're holding us up." She says this to my face with no awkwardness. Though her words bite, she's handing them to me as no more than facts. It's a relief, in a way. I know where I stand with her.

I'd like to leave myself behind, too.

"It's getting dark," Jaxon says. "And with the rain...we should finish that shelter."

I hold my right hand up. Sure enough, drops spatter onto my skin and start to pool. I've had enough of water. It would be good to have a dry place to rest.

"It's already way too dark to finish. I can't build what I can't see." Joy's voice is tight. "We're going to get soaked."

I tip my head back to check out the sky. Sure enough, through the rain, it looks like deep night. But there must be light coming from somewhere because—in spite of Joy's complaint—I'm not having any problem seeing across the clearing.

"I'll help. I'll go into the woods and collect more branches. I'll—"

Joy cuts me off. "Are you still hyped up on superzeitgeber? There's no way you can see well enough to do that."

Somehow, I can. I try to describe what I'm seeing to Jaxon and Joy. To me, it's more like twilight. All the shapes around me—trees and leaves and bushes and boulders—are distinct but without detail. That's all I need to find my way around the edge of the clearing and a few steps into the tree line.

Jaxon and Joy follow me closely, without question. We're all too brain-weary, I think, to analyze what I'm doing or how I'm doing it. That's for later. For now, I find long low branches and crack them off tree trunks. I scan the forest floor and pry up moist, mossy sheets of bark. I hand each piece over to Jaxon and Joy, who accept the burdens wordlessly. When their arms are beyond full, I lead the way back to the pile they started and we dump everything I've found on top. Then, it's time to build.

They can't see a thing, so it's only by touch that Jaxon chooses branches and Joy holds them steady while I maneuver them into place. I prop the three sturdiest branches into a tripod shape, then weave in smaller limbs and twigs until I've made something that looks like a three-sided tent. I plug the open spaces with handfuls of moss and cover them with arched slabs of bark.

The shelter is wobbly and prickly and small. If a wind kicks up, it will tip and tumble away. But it's dry. And it holds the three of us. Well, the four of us. I come in last, pushing Dublin ahead of me. He's awake now but a bit unsteady on his paws, and I wonder if he drank the river water too. He wedges himself between Jaxon and me and curls up tight beside me with his head on my lap.

Jaxon pulls off his jacket and shoves it toward me. "To cover the gap," he says. I nod, though he can't see me, and twist around to cover the tent's entryway so the rain can't drift in. His jacket will get drenched. The act is one hundred percent Jaxon, looking out for all of us instead of just himself.

After that, we stay quiet, breathing into the night air.

I watch Joy. For her eyes, I know, it's too dark to see me, though I'm only a few feet away. She sits with her hands clenched into fists in front of her.

I wish she would say something to me. Some heartfelt acknowledgement like, "Hey, Singer, we couldn't have built this shelter without you. Right now, without you, we'd be out in the rain and totally miserable." Or just, "Turns out it's not so bad to have you around."

She closes her eyes. Maybe the double darkness makes her feel safe and invisible. Or maybe she has simply forgotten that I can still see. Either way, right in front of me, she reaches out slowly and runs her fingers down Jaxon's arm until she finds his hand, which she takes shakily into her own.

I turn away, not wanting to witness her vulnerability.

What happens next is because of that, because of me giving Joy one small moment of space.

As I turn, I lean back and my shoulder bumps the inside wall of our shelter. I hear something slide, catch, slide again and hit the ground with a muted clink. Dublin lifts his muzzle off my lap and tilts his head.

I feel around behind me, thinking I'll find a piece of bark that I'll need to wedge back into place. What I catch hold of, instead, is something that is flat and smooth as driftwood. I bring my hand close to my face to see what I've got. It looks exactly like a leaf.

Even in the deep shadow here inside the shelter, I can tell that the leaf is scarlet red. The detail is flawless, with dark veins running in V patterns out to each tip. It could be the real thing—except that it feels like it's made of glossy plastic. Though it's paper thin, I don't think it's fragile. It's so perfectly crafted that I could imagine it in a museum display case.

No one else has seen this yet. My secret, I think. Something beautiful in all this mess and weariness that's just for me. I curl my fingers around the leaf, believing that somehow I can claim it and hide it. But at my touch, one spot on the leaf sinks beneath my fingertip.

I nearly drop it.

The sensation was exactly like pushing a button.

I've done something, started something, because now a pale but steady beam of light shoots out of one tip of the leaf.

Slowly I pass my other hand into the light's path. A circle of illumination appears on my palm. The circle is filled with dark squiggles and shapes that are lined up in rows. It takes me a moment, but then I get it. The squiggles are letters.

"Singer, what is that?" Jaxon's voice hitches.

Joy blinks. In their world of nighttime darkness, the sudden glow from the leaf must look eerily bright.

"I'm not sure," I say. "I think I found some kind of projector." I lean in closer. "These are words. Actual words. From someone... here in the TimeTilter."

And I begin to read.

TimeTilter

Sonia Ellis

PART II

ILLUSION:

a thing that produces a false
perception of reality

Sonia Ellis

Chapter 1
Dram

Is anybody out there?

There are three of us here:

Me. My name is Dram Moore. I'm fifteen.

Delia Moore. My sister. Seven years old.

Royaltee. That's the only name she'll give. Says she's fourteen. Not sure I believe much of anything she says.

I'd tell you how long we've been in the TimeTilter, but that is the joke, right? Time is different here. It feels like a long long time.

I've spent a lot of that time thinking and putting this whole thing together in my head. Now that I've found a way to tell it, I am going to start at the beginning. If I don't tell it in order, I'll leave things out that you might need to know.

This is what happened to Delia and me and how we got here, from the beginning.

We are both adopted. So we're brother and sister, just not by blood. There were eight other kids in my family. Which makes ten altogether. Some adopted, some fostered. I will say it bluntly: That was too many. It'll be no surprise when I tell you there was never enough money, never enough of anything—food, clothes, medicine— to go around. We shared shoes and we pinched toothpaste tubes down to nothing and we fought over any tiny space we could call our own. Harley, the oldest—they kicked him out when he turned seventeen. Then Riley. I was smart enough to see who was up next. Didn't wait to be kicked out. I left and took Delia too. They won't be missing her.

(Sorry, Del, but it's true. You were too much trouble from the start.)

Part of me didn't want to leave the others behind, and part of me didn't want to take Delia with me because of where I was going—or, I mean to say, because I didn't know where I was going. We ended up at a bus station and I told people I lost my wallet and Delia put on her sad lost face and we got a lot of money that way. But the bus station was small. I got the idea to go to a train station in the city. A lot of people there, and they didn't always watch their stuff and their cash. So I brought Delia into the unknown where we lived day to day and got by through conning and stealing. Which means I'm not fit to be the big brother of a seven-year-old. I wanted better for her than I could do for myself. But I guess she would have ended up kicked out of the house anyway and at least now we have each other.

(Del, don't listen to this next part, because I'm going to tell some facts.)

When you first see Delia you think she's cute and small and calm. The first two are true but the last one is not. She sees or hears something—I never know what—and the sight or sound fires up a memory that should be kept dark, and then I lose her. She screams. Flat-out screams with so much rage it hurts to look at her. People hear that once, they don't forget it.

And there's the other thing. Delia draws. She steals pens and paint and little kids' crayons—right out of their hands—and draws on sidewalks and walls and benches. It's all shapes that don't come together to look like anything real to me, but it means something big to her. And what she draws...well, it catches people's attention and they want to see more. They want to watch her make these wild sweeps of noisy color that bunch your heart up in your chest and make your eyes water.

So Delia can't hide in a crowd like I can. That's why we had to keep moving, city to city.

(Okay, Dellie Bellie, uncover your ears now. I know you were listening anyway.)

I saw an ad for the TimeTilter in a train station we passed through one night. High on the wall, a poster that must have been ten feet tall.

An adventure beyond anything you can imagine.
Bend the Rules
Stretch Time
...and be home before dinner

That's what the ad said—I still can see it in my head. From the moment I saw the words, I was hooked. Everywhere we went from then on, I looked out for more news about the TimeTilter.

I've always been a gamer—as much as I could be without money to buy games and without anything to play them on. I played Order of Destiny a few times on a phone that Harley had for exactly four days before he sold it. After that, I played the game in my head for about a million hours. So the TimeTilter sounded like something out of a dream to me, something that was too good to be real. I wanted to get in that place and stretch time so wide it would never bounce back. Though we were always on the move, I kept circling back to the ad, staring at it while Delia drew on the station floor in wider and wider circles.

We came back to that place again and again, and then it was one time too many. I will keep this part short because I don't like to remember it though it stays bitter in my head. We were asleep outside, behind the station, on a bench that no one else ever sits on. We were attacked. For no reason I could imagine, because we have nothing that anybody else would want except for a few dollars. I have never been in a fight, but I did what I could to keep Delia behind me and take the worst of it myself.

That's where Angelie Bonneville found us. She yelled for the attack to stop and right away it did. That made no sense at the time.

Delia and I both ended up hurt. Angelie picked us up, one under each arm like we weighed nothing, and said she would take us someplace safe. I never questioned her. Another time that I was not the best big brother for Delia. Then we found out that what Angelie meant by "someplace safe" was the TimeTilter, exactly the place I'd been wanting so badly to be. But the truth is that Angelie found me first. She knew well ahead of time that it wouldn't take much talking to sign me up.

What I am saying is that it was not all by chance

Royaltee has her own story. She doesn't talk much, but here is what I got from her. She is a foster kid too; she lived on a commune. I didn't know what that was, until she told me it's where a bunch of people live together and share whatever they have. That sounds a lot like my home. Except I guess her people had enough of everything. Even so, Royaltee says she always wanted to leave and then one day she did, in the darkest part of the night. Things are never very dark around Royaltee because her sweater has the brightest white shooting stars stitched all over it. She says you can find your way by looking at constellations in the sky, and that is what the stars on her sweater stand for: finding her way back to someone, though she won't say who.

(Delia says I should tell you this: she found out, from seeing a tag on that sweater, that Royaltee's name isn't real. It's made out of the mixed up letters of her given name—Taylor. That's one example of why I don't always believe Royaltee.)

Anyway, Royaltee said that on the commune, people always come and go, so no one was wondering where she was.

Once we were here, Delia and I—and Royaltee too, I suppose— jumped right in, thinking we were so smart and so lucky.

Now there is one more thing I want to tell you, whoever might be out there in the same mess as we are.

After I woke up from being prepped for the TimeTilter, my eyes hurt and wouldn't stop hurting for a while. I didn't mind that but there is something else. You won't want to believe it but you should. Here it is: I can see things that have already happened. I see them again, like I'm watching them in real time. I can see places I've been, exactly as they were. Like this: right now, if I want, I can see Delia drawing on the train station floor—every dusty color and every gritty bit of dirt. I can hear all the noises that go with it, too, like the train rumbling under my feet and the buzz from the speaker announcing another arrival from Philadelphia on Track 10. Every detail. I can see back in time.

Which is weird enough. But there's something else I keep seeing. It's my foster brother Harley's phone. One time when I borrowed it, I went on GameSqueal and—well, first, you probably do not know what that is. GameSqueal posts gaming news that disappears in two minutes. If you don't catch it when they post it, that is too bad, it is gone. I saw one post. I can see it right now, in front of my eyes. Just one sentence.

It said: "Collusia insiders leak existence of possible exit problem with TimeTilter technology."

I don't know what that means. Except that it's bad for any of us inside this place, if there's really a problem with getting out.

That's all I have got for now. Push the button and hold it down—I figured out that's how you can record a message. If you find this and want to say something back.

(I don't know, Del. I don't know if anyone else is really out there.)

Delia's Portfolio:

collusia.com/timetiltertesters/delia

Dram's Portfolio:

collusia.com/timetiltertesters/dram

Royaltee's Portfolio:

collusia.com/timetiltertesters/royaltee

Chapter 2
Singer

After I finish reading Dram's message, Joy and Jaxon don't say anything right away.

Even though I was the one speaking Dram's words aloud, it's his voice that I hear lingering in the dark. Everything he said seemed so completely honest, with nothing held back. If he appeared suddenly inside this shaky shelter, I feel like I would already know him.

So much of his story is bizarre and at the same time bizarrely familiar to what Joy, Jaxon and I have been through. But out of his entire message—all the questions and craziness and doubts— there's one particular part that keeps pushing itself to the front of my mind. What he said about not taking care of Delia like a big brother should, of not being good enough. I know that feeling. I know it deeply.

I wish that Dram were really standing right in front of me so that I could let him know I understand. There's a story I'd tell him, as honestly as he told his.

For a little while, I'd say, I had a friend named Callie Kent. She ran the fastest of any girl in fifth grade, and I ran the slowest. It didn't make sense that we were best friends when our lives didn't keep the same pace. But she was the engine and I was the caboose of a two-car train that somehow stayed linked together. The first time that Callie came over to my house, she walked through the living room and into the kitchen and then up to my bedroom, all the while staring around like she was in a museum.

"Your house is so...quiet," she said. And I got the feeling that she meant more than sound, that the "quiet" encompassed color, movement and even emotion. My house was always in order: shoes lined up by the door, magazines centered on the coffee table, spoons and forks and knives grouped separately in the dishwasher caddy. "We take care of the things we value," my mother said. That's why, back then, I believed I was valued: because I was taken care of. My parents bought me clothes that were lined up neatly on their hangers, they helped me with my homework so it was never handed in late, and they kept sliced apples and chocolate milk cartons stocked in the refrigerator for my snacks.

When I finally got to see Callie's house, the first thing I noticed was that nothing was in order. The messiness didn't come from dirt, crumbs or dog hair. It was more the mess of chaos. Callie tossed her backpack and sneakers onto a tumbling pile by the front door, swung her coat over the back of a kitchen chair, and shoved haphazard piles of folded laundry to the middle of the table to make room for placemats and dinner plates. Callie and her family talked on top of one another in a way that was hard to follow, but pretty soon I wasn't listening anyway. I couldn't take my eyes off the walls. It seemed like every one of them—above the mantel, up the staircase, along the hall—was covered with photos of Callie and her family. The photos were as chaotic as the house: quick snapshots with messy backgrounds and silly faces. But if I had wanted to see what Callie looked like at any age over the past eight years, somewhere in this house, on some wall, there would be a photograph to show me. I stared hard, picture by picture, noting the constant curve of Mrs. Kent's arm around Callie and her little brother Liam, the way Mr. Kent's whole face seemed widened with happiness around his kids. Callie's home was as much of a museum to me as mine was to her.

That same night, after my parents were asleep, I got up, slid out of my bedroom and began a slow and careful tour of the house on my own. I had never noticed before how empty the walls were. Not empty of anything, just empty of me. There were photo collages of my parents running triathlons together. Lots of those. There were framed ribbons won by the golden retrievers. Lots of those too. But none of me. I ignored the walls, then, and began to claw through drawers, inside boxes on high shelves, and finally in the deep dark backs of closets. There was not a moment in my last eight years that had been saved and framed. As if all of my life up to this point simply didn't exist.

I finally understood: with my dragging leg that would never let me run a marathon or win a ribbon, what about me, after all, was worth preserving?

So I know what it's like to feel that you're not good enough. But I would like to tell Dram it's not true for him. He didn't leave Delia behind. And he stood between her and an ugly fight. That's worth something.

It takes two more read-throughs of Dram's communication and hours of talking, with each of us nodding off into sleep at some point, before we see the first artificial light of dawn and decide what's going to happen next.

I argue for staying right here and searching for Dram, Delia and Royaltee. It makes sense to me that they'd stay close to this spot. It's where they left the message. It's true, we're invisible to each other because we're in different time perceptions. But we might bump into them by chance—and that physical contact would bring us all together.

Joy, as I could have predicted, votes for action. She's taken hold of two of Dram's words—exit problem—and won't let go. "Staying here is a waste of time. I told you before, we need to get out of here." She shifts restlessly. "I think the exit problem is that this place is making all of us lose it."

"You're right." Jaxon puts a hand on her arm like he wants to keep her from bolting out of our sight. "I know you don't trust Angelie, but I think she might have been trying to give us the same warning. We should keep going."

After my overdosing on the superzeitgeber, I can't deny that the TimeTilter has been messing with my mind. More than that: I'm starting to wonder if being in here is affecting me in other ways. I've never felt this weary before. My muscles feel more drained all the time. I haven't mentioned anything to Joy and Jaxon. I've been enough of a liability to them as it is.

So we're doing this Joy's way. We'll keep going.

I get the job of leaving our own message for Dram. Just like he instructed, I press down on the nearly hidden button that I first found by accident. This time, in the light, I see how it works. The vivid color on the leaf fades until it's transparent—I can see right through it to the ground. But there are four little icons floating inside the leaf and after some experimenting, I figure them out. I can Select, Play, Record and Delete. That's it. I don't find any other messages, from Dram or anyone else. I'm thankful for the Delete icon, because my first recording is the exact opposite of Dram's careful chronological message. It rambles all over the place.

My second try is better. I tell him everything: who we are, where we came from and how we ended up here. I tell him how Jaxon can see things that are far away. And how I've been able to see in the dark. We've barely acknowledged that ourselves, much less made any sense of it. Dram's altered sight—seeing things from his past—is even stranger. He didn't say there was anything different about Delia's or Royaltee's sight. Joy hasn't mentioned any changes either. I'm not exactly sure why that gives me a little internal jump of satisfaction. It shouldn't. My eyes working differently—that can't be for any reason that's good.

When I finish recording, I slip the leaf back on the branch it came from. That's what we agreed, so that Dram could find it again if he comes back to this place.

When we leave the shelter, the rain—which was never much more than a drizzle, anyway—has stopped. As Joy and Jaxon head out of the clearing and into the woods, still in sight but with their backs to me, I pause and look back. The leaf is my one connection to Dram. To someone whose voice is so forthright and whose emotions seem so similar to my own. I can't leave that behind.

I grab the leaf and stuff it into the back pocket of my jeans, and we move on.

Chapter 3
Dram

Singer. Are you real? Are you really out there?

Delia and I found your message. We read it like thirsty people drink water, not wanting to stop. Which makes me remember, we won't be drinking from the river now. You said you had a bad time with that. We will be careful.

You didn't say where you are in the TimeTilter. Though I didn't either. Because I don't know where I am. What if we were walking side by side all this time, no more than an arm's length apart, separated only by our perceptions? I wonder if this is the same as looking for something that's right in front of you and not seeing it, because your brain has already decided it's not there. But I believe you're there. Your words are real. Everything you told us, I see it as plainly in my head as if I had lived through it with you.

You asked me some questions but I don't have any answers. Just more questions to give back to you. First I'll tell you that your warning about the shadows in the swamp came too late. We passed through the swamp in the dark and the silence and didn't know that anything was wrong until we came out the other side. Then Royaltee said that something had happened to her, that something had grabbed her insides and shook her until she felt like she was on fire and then let her go. But like I told you before, I'm not always sure if she tells the truth. It sounded like a story she could tell that no one could disprove. So I left it alone. But if you've seen them too...

What do you think the shadows are? Have you seen them outside the swamp?

I have more to say but I have to stop now. Royaltee is on the move again. It's hard to keep us together. Sometimes I think she wants to get separated from Delia and me. Not because we're in her way. Just because we're trying so hard to get out.

Before I go I have to tell you one other thing: I never really believed someone would find my message.

(No, Delia, I didn't lie to you. I just wanted you to have hope.)

Now we have it. Hope. We don't have to figure this out by ourselves.

We're not alone.

Chapter 4
Singer

I'm not leading the way anymore. Joy takes that job, while Jaxon keeps watching far ahead for arrows. He spots two more of them, but who knows if we should be following them or not. Maybe they just point in circles to keep us spiraling around the TimeTilter forever. Each time we reach one of the arrows, Joy chooses our route, and as far as I know her choices are completely random.

Jaxon looks back over his shoulder every few minutes to make sure I'm still in sight. He and Joy are exhausted, I can tell, but I seem to be fading faster. I'm leaning on Dublin more and more. And I look back over my own shoulder every few minutes to make sure I don't see any shadows. I wonder if they could be some sort of virtual border patrols, meant to keep us from running into the outer walls of the TimeTilter. I guess that sort of makes sense. Except for the part where the shadow traveled through Joy's body. There was nothing virtual about that. The pain on her face was stark and real. I wonder what it felt like when it happened, but she won't talk about it. There's a part of me that admires Joy's ability to close herself up like that. Like she doesn't want or need anyone else's opinion.

We're out of the forest again. No more swamp or cliff or river. Instead, the land rises and falls in an endless repetition of stubby hills and shallow trenches. It's tough and tiring to cross. But still undeniably breathtaking. The grass on the hills looks like the fur on a wolf: soft, thick and a feral mix of grey and brown. For the first time, I'm glad I lost my sneakers because the grass feels soothing under my feet. Dublin is happier when we reach the bottom of each hill. The trenches are sliced down the middle by narrow ruts of ice-white water. Dublin dips his paws in the water and rolls on his back until his whole body is dripping and muddy.

"Nice try," I tell him. "But a golden retriever will never look like a wolf."

As we trudge along, I keep the leaf curled in my hand so that Jaxon can't see it whenever he turns around to check my progress. Every few minutes I sneak a peek at the leaf as surreptitiously as I can. I run my finger across the shiny surface, which feels cool and calming against my palm. A few times I bring the leaf up to my face and hold it against my cheek.

That's how I finally notice that the leaf has changed color.

The scarlet red pulses to an even brighter shade and then abruptly fades to transparency. I peer at it quickly. Next to the Select icon, I spot a tiny word in black that says "New."

It's another message from Dram. I didn't expect that. How could he have sent it when I have the leaf? It doesn't make sense, but at this moment I can't make myself think about it. I just need to find out what he wrote.

It takes me nearly an hour—a TimeTilter hour, anyway—to read the message. I take it in slowly, word by word, so that Jaxon and Joy don't notice. By the time I get to the end, I have the whole thing practically memorized. I can hear all of it replaying in my head. I like the way Dram is looking out for Delia and keeping the two of them connected with Royaltee. He's right; we could be near each other and never know it. That fact comforts and frustrates me at the same time.

Dram said he didn't know where he was or how we could find each other. But I have an idea about how we could figure that out. Each environment that we've passed through has had something unique about it: the shimmering colors of the moss, the twistedness of the trees, the bumpiness of the hills. So what if I asked Dram to stay in one spot and describe everything about it, down to the tiniest feature? Maybe we could find him that way. The TimeTilter is huge, I know. But it's not infinite. And we have time.

As soon as I have that last thought, I realize that I am actually entirely wrong. Time may be exactly what we don't have. We're supposed to be hurrying toward the exit. I'm glad I didn't mention my idea to Jaxon and Joy. As usual, it would probably just have led us into trouble.

But if I'm not sharing that, I think with a stubborn shrug, then I won't share Dram's message, either. After all, I'm not even supposed to have the leaf with me, and I'm really not interested in hearing Joy explode if she finds out. And anyway, Dram didn't say anything she needs to know.

I want this to be mine alone. For just a little while longer, I promise myself.

I keep the leaf shielded in my palm, out of sight to anyone but me.

Chapter 5
Jaxon

Jaxon had never been a keeper of secrets. Bad news, he always figured, felt better when it was shared, and good news—well, what was the point of holding that in?

But this time, probably for the first time in his life, Jaxon decided not to share.

It was happening again. That weird sensation of seeing something that wasn't actually in front of his face.

"Look at the roots on this tree!" Joy was walking a good ten feet ahead of him and blocking his view when she said this. Yet Jaxon could see the beautiful braided roots in precise detail well before he caught up with Joy and saw them for real. It felt like he was viewing things briefly through Joy's eyes.

Then it happened again as Joy rounded a bend in the trail slightly ahead of him. For a fleeting moment he saw the section of trail ahead of Joy before he reached it: the stubbly golden moss, the spiraling lantern light, the tree trunks arching like question marks.

Even without this mysterious new perception, it was already strange and unsettling that he'd been spotting all those distant arrows when nobody else could. And that Singer could see at night. And that Dram, apparently, could see pieces of his past. So Angelie had tampered with their vision. When had that happened? Singer had said she was already unconscious when Angelie found her, and she woke up with her eyes burning—which she thought was from the fire. Jaxon, on the other hand, had simply agreed to be prepped for the TimeTilter without having any idea what that meant. He was put under and woke up with the same red and watering eyes. Joy must have gone through the same thing, though at the time he'd thought the surgeon was just stitching up all her injuries from the explosion.

That took care of *when* their sight was altered. But how and why? Those questions were too complicated for Jaxon to tackle when his thoughts felt so slow and muddled.

There was one thought, at least, that he wasn't confused about: he would not tell Joy about seeing things through her eyes. Joy hadn't mentioned any changes in her own sight. Jaxon could imagine her reaction to finding out that he was more or less hacking her vision.

"We're doomed."

A few seconds passed before Jaxon realized that the voice was Joy's in the here and now. She had pulled up short and was staring ahead. This time, Jaxon hadn't seen it coming. In front of them rose a tall tangled hedge. Its branches were woven together too tightly to see through and covered with rows of needle-sharp thorns.

"How are we supposed to get past this?" Joy asked.

Jaxon looked left and right. The wall stretched as far as he could see, so trying to get around it would probably be a waste of time. "Cut through it, maybe?"

"With what, our bare hands?" Joy gently touched the hedge. When she pulled away, her fingers were covered with tiny pinpricks of blood. She wiped her hand on her jacket and shook her head.

Singer and Dublin, side by side as always, caught up to them. Singer sank to the ground with a heavy breath. "Another obstacle," she said. "I hate to say it, but, you know, it's kind of pretty."

Jaxon cast a quick glance at Singer. She was serious. He turned back to the brambles. Up close, he could see what she was talking about. Strands of cobwebs looped and crisscrossed among the branches, creating intricate lacy patterns.

"Those are made by orb-weaver spiders," she said. "I read about them. See how some of the webs are shaped like a bicycle wheel?"

The strands were so thin they were nearly invisible, but from certain angles they shimmered faintly. Yes, in wheel shapes. And pretty, sort of. But the cobwebs couldn't hide the fact that the hedge was armored with thorns and impenetrable.

"Maybe there's a trapdoor, like at the river," Joy said. "So we could go underneath it."

"Okay then, that's a plan," Jaxon agreed. "Let's search."

After what felt like forever later, Jaxon regretted his suggestion. They had searched methodically, each of them covering a long stretch of ground along the hedge, where they scraped and shifted dirt, weeds and rocks. Now Jaxon's hands and arms were muddy and scratched up. And all for nothing. Their digging hadn't turned up any secret door or tunnel.

Joy kept at it, inspecting the ground further and further away from the hedge. But it looked like Singer was done. She lay on her back in the grass, staring up at the sky. Jaxon stretched out beside her.

"Just when we think we're getting somewhere...we're not," he said. "Look at Joy, though. She's really givin' it socks."

Singer glanced sideways at him. "Giving it socks? What's that—Irish or something?"

"It means, you know, really going for it." Jaxon half-smiled. "She won't give up."

"Yeah, I noticed that about her. She doesn't let things drop."

Jaxon felt his face redden. Singer must have noticed Joy's attitude toward him ever since they entered the TimeTilter. "She's tough," he said. "She's been that way as long as I've known her."

Singer looked back up at the sky, giving him space. "So how long *have* you known her? I don't know much of anything about you and Joy."

"True enough." Jaxon kept his eyes fixed on Joy, who was still in sight but out of hearing range. "Anyway, there's not much to tell about me. My dad died when I was five. I don't really remember him. My mom always had a lot of...problems. Things got worse and she took off when I was ten. I was put into foster care. I got moved around a lot, but I had some good homes."

Singer nodded. "And Joy?"

"I don't know what happened to Joy's mother. But she told me her dad was really sick for a long time, and he lost his job. So things weren't easy for them. Then he passed away when Joy was thirteen. That's why she ended up in the foster system."

"And that's where Angelie found you?"

"Yeah." Jaxon paused. "Well, no, not exactly. Joy hated being in foster care. She wanted to take care of herself. She ran away, and I ran with her. We were staying in an old house, where no one lived anymore. That's the house that blew up. And that's when Angelie showed up."

Singer nodded again, accepting his story without comment.

"Your turn," Jaxon said. "Were you in a foster home?"

"No. But I ran away too," Singer said briefly. "To save this one." She patted Dublin, who was slowly nosing his way between them.

"So you have parents. You lived with them, before you ran away?"

"Yes. I know what you're saying. Having a family and running away from it was thoughtless and ungrate—"

"That's *not* what I'm saying," Jaxon cut her off. "No judgments here. I just mean, there's someone out there who will come looking for you. Right?

Singer shrugged. "Eventually, I guess, yes. But they're away. For three days. And they probably won't call to check on me while they're gone." She paused. "Three days out there is...how long in here?"

"I don't know. Weeks? Months? Whatever. It could be too late." Jaxon fell silent. He wished he hadn't started this conversation.

Singer exhaled slowly. It looked like she'd had enough talking too. Dublin, as if sensing Jaxon's bleak mood, inched a little closer. Jaxon wound his fingers into Dublin's soft fur, just like Singer always did. He scratched Dublin gently while the dog snuffled against his arm. It *was* sort of calming.

"Look up there." Singer elbowed Jaxon and pointed skyward. "Someone messed up."

"What?"

"It's just, everything about this place is designed so...carefully. The trees and the leaves and all that, I know they look odd, but they're all balanced. Like they fit together exactly where they need to be. But look." She pointed to one patch of sky. "That cloud. It's casting a shadow on the sky instead of on the ground."

Singer was right. The cloud threw a faint grey shadow onto the sky, as if the sun were lighting it from below. Definitely, someone had messed up. Jaxon allowed himself a small internal tic of satisfaction. Somehow this tiny bit of imperfection made the TimeTilter seem a tiny bit less real and less terrifying. Like how a little flaw, Jaxon thought, could make a person seem less annoying and more likeable.

The cloud drifted realistically in the sky, passing behind a tree that stretched high above them. From this angle, Jaxon could see the craggy bark on the undersides of all the branches.

And he could see the arrow.

Jaxon bounced to his feet, craning his neck for a better view. No, he wasn't imagining it. The same arrow as all the others, carved neatly into the bark. It was pointing up and across the hedge.

"Joy! Singer! Over here!" Jaxon ran to where Joy was crouched by the hedge and pulled her to the tree. "See the arrow? No, sorry, of course you can't, it's too high up. But it means we've been thinking about this the wrong way. We're supposed to go *over* the hedge."

Joy stared at him. "I thought of that already. But I didn't say anything—because it didn't make sense. How are we supposed to climb...uh...twenty feet up a tree?"

"I don't know. But the arrow must mean something." Jaxon walked slowly around the tree. The bark was thick and rough-edged. A yellow, spongy-looking fungus circled the base of the tree, piled up like stacks of pancakes. Jaxon poked at one of the pancakes. It didn't yield.

Singer crouched down and carefully pried up a slice of fungus. She ran her finger along one edge, where the fungus had been attached to the tree. When she flipped the fungus over, Jaxon saw a stem that was shaped sort of like a hook. Singer looked at Jaxon and raised her eyebrows.

Jaxon got it right away. He took the fungus from Singer, lifted it higher up the tree and hitched it into the gap between pieces of bark. It jutted out from the trunk—just like a small step.

Jaxon tapped the step. Its outer tip oscillated up and down like the end of a diving board, but the hook held firmly in place. With an arched-eyebrow look tossed at Joy and Singer, Jaxon raised his foot and put his weight slowly on the step, testing its strength. The fungus started a slow and comical downward bend, and Jaxon quickly slammed his foot closer to the tree's trunk. This time, the step held.

Jaxon hopped down, threw his arms up in victory and took Joy by the shoulders. "Next time you have a thought, Bronagh," he said in mock reproval, "don't keep it to yourself. Look where this is taking us—up the tree and over the hedge."

"Yeah, we'll see." Joy shook loose from him, and Jaxon felt his stomach twist. She crouched down and wrenched up more pieces of fungus, tossing aside the longer plates that were more likely to bend. As Jaxon and Singer watched, she hooked each piece into the bark, starting near the base of the tree and ending as high as she could reach. Then she began to climb their offbeat staircase. The steps took her weight and she was quickly above Jaxon's head. She hooked more steps into the tree above her and kept going, rising slowly and steadily until she was even with the top of the hedge.

"What do you see?" Jaxon yelled up at her.

"Good news, I think." Joy huffed with the exertion of pulling herself higher. "The hedge isn't very wide. And there's a tree on the other side. If I can crawl across this branch..."

"Wait!" Jaxon could hear the edge of panic in his own voice when he yelled again. "If you go over the other side, we won't be able to see you."

"So hurry. Get up here."

Jaxon put his foot on the first step and then caught himself. He looked back at Singer, who gazed at him steadily.

"I can't climb that, especially not with Dublin," she said. "And I'm not leaving him behind. So go ahead. You'll move faster without me."

"I'm not leaving *you* behind. I promise that. Neither of you." Jaxon gave Dublin a quick scratch behind his fleecy drooping ears. "Look, here's what I'll do. I'll just climb up to where Joy is, so I can keep her in sight. Then she can search for a way down the other side. In the meantime, you and I will figure out a way to get you up there. Okay?"

Singer nodded briefly, as if she didn't quite believe him.

Jaxon drew a breath and turned away. He didn't want to leave Singer here on the ground, but he could see Joy shimmying up to a higher branch that stretched over the hedge.

"Hey, hold on," Singer said. "You should take more pieces with you, in case Joy needs them to get down." Singer bent down and something bright red tumbled to the ground in front of her.

Jaxon reached for it, but Singer was faster. She scooped up whatever it was and slid it into her back pocket.

"Singer, what was that?"

She shook her head. "Nothing. Just...nothing."

"Jaxon, come on," Joy shouted at him. "What's going on down there?"

Jaxon took a breath. That scarlet color...it looked exactly the same as the leaf Singer had found in the shelter. The one with Dram's message. He fixed his eyes on Singer's face, which she kept carefully blank.

"Singer," he said. "Did you..."

"Seriously! Jaxon?" Joy called impatiently. "I can't hear you. What happened?"

"I think," he said as loudly but as evenly as he could, "that Singer kept the leaf."

A few beats of absolute silence passed. Then Singer muttered something Jaxon couldn't hear and slowly pulled the leaf out of her pocket. She held it in her hand, palm up, where it shimmered boldly.

From thirty feet overhead, Joy inhaled harshly. She must have seen the leaf. "What are you doing with that?"

Jaxon could feel Joy's anger raining down. Singer opened her mouth twice but no words came out. Her struggle to come up with an answer was almost too painful to watch.

Joy wasn't finished. "You were supposed to leave that behind. So you just ignored what we all agreed to and decided to keep it to yourself?" Joy's voice cut between the branches, louder with each breath she took. "What were you thinking? What if he came back there to find our message? Now he'll never know we're here. Of all the completely selfish—"

"He sent another message," Singer said.

"What?"

Singer tilted her head back, facing Joy's fury. "We got another message from Dram. There was nothing in it to help us. But it means he found a way to contact us again."

"What it means, Singer," Joy spit, "is that you only care about yourself. We're supposed to be a team, which I didn't even want to be, but we got this far together and now you're keeping secrets and you don't get to decide what's important and what isn't."

Jaxon turned to Singer. She stood motionless, the leaf resting in her outstretched palm, her eyes welling. Jaxon had no idea why she had really kept it but couldn't find any anger inside him. Whatever was going on, it didn't feel likely that Singer meant to betray them. Still, something bothered him. If Dram didn't have the leaf, how had he recorded another message?

Jaxon sighed. He wouldn't fuel Joy's outrage with the question just yet. He shifted back a few feet, trying to get a better look at her. She was inching her way even further along a fat branch that curved over the top of the hedge.

"Guess what, Singer," Joy called out. "I can see things a lot more clearly from up here. And you know what I see? It's you holding us back instead of helping us get out of here."

Joy was nearly over the hedge. Jaxon put a foot back on the first step on the tree. "Joy, don't go any further. I won't be able to see you."

"Then let's go. I am so done with this place."

Jaxon climbed up a few more feet as Joy pushed on. She squirrel-hopped recklessly to another branch, dipping nearly out of his sight.

Jaxon climbed faster, step to step, until he reached the spot where Joy had perched seconds ago. At this moment, he could see Singer below him on one side of the hedge and Joy on the other. They couldn't see each other. He was the single connection that kept them in the same perception.

Joy dropped to a lower branch and then to the ground. If he followed her—even leaned a bit her way—he would lose Singer.

But if he turned back, Joy would be out of sight and gone.

No one was going to make this decision for him. However Jaxon chose, the link among the three of them would be broken.

Someone would be left alone.

Chapter 6
Monet

Monet could not shake Hunter Slope out of her mind.

When he'd left her office, with a promise to contact her again within the next couple of days, Hunter had taken the vision enhancement document with him. Moments later, Monet realized she should have asked for a copy, but it was too late: she'd searched the nearby hallways and stairwells, but he was gone.

The uneasy jitters in her body grew throughout the morning. She checked in with four other employees in her department, fishing cautiously for information. None of them mentioned anything more than the usual worn-out company gossip and complaints about overlong work hours and incompetent managers. Then again, none of them had her level of access to the TimeTilter.

Monet could not shake the feeling that she had to talk to Hunter again—soon. She needed to find out what else he knew. And more than that, she needed an ally. It was miserable feeling this alone.

Monet rarely left her desk for lunch. Today she should have stayed in her office doing more research on solar electric systems.

But every time she sat down in front of her computer, she just popped back up again to pace the room and reconsider every nuance of her conversation with Hunter. Finally she gave up. She looked up Hunter's location in the company directory, tossed her laptop and phone into her bag and headed out.

Room 314 in the Solein Building was a ten-minute walk and two flights up. "Hunter Slope" was engraved on a plaque to the left of the closed door. Monet rapped sharply. No answer. She knocked more decisively, three brisk strikes.

"Hunter? Are you there?"

No answer.

Monet leaned down to look at the gap between the floor and the bottom of the door. Dark. She placed one hand on the silver door handle and pressed down. The door swung open and Monet stepped into what must have been Hunter Slope's office as recently as this morning but now was obviously not.

The room was bare except for a desk, a chair, a wastebasket and a bookshelf that were all completely empty. Dust on the bookshelves marked the ghostly outlines of books and binders. Monet sniffed in the dry, unsettled smell that comes from the movement of furniture and boxes. She walked over to the desk and opened every drawer. They were all predictably bare. She gave the wastebasket a kick and watched it roll away.

Hunter wasn't here. And Monet didn't need a memo to tell her that he wasn't coming back.

She looked around the room again. It really was bare, without a stray sticky note or paper clip left in any corner. Even the whiteboard on the wall had been wiped clean. Well, nearly clean. Monet walked closer to the whiteboard. She could see remnants of green, orange, blue and red marker swipes. Apparently Hunter liked to color code. Monet leaned in to examine the leftover marks. Although someone had been pretty diligent with the eraser, she could make out two words. One looked something like **SHIVE...R**. Shiver? But some letters were missing. The tops of the letters were chopped off the second word, but Monet projected each line and curve in her head. What she came up with, weirdly, was **STARFISH.**

That was no help at all.

After one more sweep, Monet decided that this room wasn't going to yield any more information.

But she did have a half-formed thought about where she could go next.

She wanted to know why she was being shut out of the TimeTilter. So where would be the best place to find the answer? Well, probably *inside* the TimeTilter.

Monet was going to have to find a way to break in.

Chapter 7
Singer

When Jaxon climbs down the tree on my side of the hedge, I feel sick with an unlikely mix of gratitude and horror.

I didn't expect Jaxon to choose that way. Watching him balance high on the branch, looking frantically between Joy and me, I thought it would be the last time I'd ever see him. I would, in fact, have bet my life on it.

But here he stands beside me, his face so strained and surprised that I'm sure he couldn't have predicted this outcome either.

"Joy!" I scream. I don't really expect a response. Being on a different time perception means being out of hearing as much as out of sight. And Jaxon let her go on alone, so I'm sure she wouldn't answer even if she did hear me.

"Why did you do that?" I shout at Jaxon. Even though Joy was ready—and pushing—to leave me behind, I'm not glad she's gone. If something goes wrong for her...that's on me. It will be my fault, because Jaxon is with me.

"I don't even know," he says, his voice soft and tenuous. "I wanted us all to stick together. We need each other. But..." Jaxon shakes his head. "She didn't see it that way. I don't know. Maybe she does have the best chance of making it out of here if she doesn't have to worry about...us."

"It's okay," I say quickly. "I know you mean *me*."

"I don't mean that. You must have noticed that Joy's been mad at me. She thinks I've made some bad decisions."

I think back to that moment in our shelter, in the dark, when Joy reached out to hold Jaxon's hand. I'm certain Joy wanted Jaxon to go with her.

"Well, one good thing is this. If she can move faster and get out of the TimeTilter, then maybe she can figure out a way to get us out too." I want to make Jaxon's face look a bit less sad, and that's the best I can come up with.

Jaxon takes my cue, adjusting his shoulders with a big breath. "Right. Enough with this olagonin' and standin' around like muppets. Let's head on."

I smile faintly. "Every time you turn on the Irish thing, I can't understand a word you're saying."

Jaxon gives me an innocent look. "I said, very distinctly I'm sure, enough with this complainin' and standin' around like fools." He turns to face me. "One thing that you have to promise me, though."

I raise my eyebrows, not sure what's coming.

"No more hiding the leaf. Okay?"

"Okay." I nod solemnly to let Jaxon know I mean it. I don't need to keep Dram's messages to myself anymore. It's time to put together every voice we have.

Although we've made the decision to keep going, neither of us is quite ready to move. I wonder if Jaxon is half hoping for Joy to reappear. He keeps looking up at the top of the hedge as if her face might pop back into view. To distract him, I start recording a message to Dram, Delia and Royaltee. I can't think of any way for us to find them. So instead, I ask them to tell us anything they know—or just imagine—about why we're in this place. I tell them how tired we are. I tell them what we plan to do next. And I tell them that we've lost Joy.

When I get to that part, Jaxon looks away and I stop recording.

"So, if Dram is getting messages to us without this leaf, I guess we should hang on to it," I say.

"I was wondering about that." Jaxon takes the leaf from me and flips it over a few times. "How do you think he recorded his last message?"

"Yeah, I've been thinking about that too. We can ask him. But I might..." I hesitate. I know Joy didn't have much faith in my ideas, and I'm not completely sure yet if Jaxon will want to hear this. But he gives me an encouraging nod. "So, okay. Look around. There are leaves everywhere, right? I'm guessing a bunch of leaf recorders have been hiding in plain sight the whole time."

"Yeah?" Jaxon stares at me, eyes narrowed. "Well, there's an easy enough way to test that theory."

He scans the ground around us. We shuffle through the leaves, kicking them high, and Jaxon plucks some down from low branches. It doesn't take long to gather a small pile of scarlet red leaves. Some are as crinkly as paper, some rubbery, some smooth as glass—and one that feels like glossy plastic.

"This one," I say. I run my fingers over the surface until I find the button I'm looking for. The leaf turns transparent and I watch as the familiar icons appear.

I start projecting Dram's message again:

Singer. Are you real? Are you really out there?

I let out a little breath of surprise that I actually got this right. Seeing his words one more time, I realize how much I've depended on this connection with Dram to keep me moving forward.

Jaxon gives me a gentle congratulatory punch on the shoulder, but I'm too excited to leave it that: I grab him in a hug and then release him to do a quick clumsy dance. For a moment at least, I can pretend that I'm not exhausted and parched and scared.

Jaxon and I each keep one of the red leaves and walk together, with Dublin between us, to the base of the tree we need to climb. Where we stop cold. Because there's still that nagging problem we haven't found the answer to.

How, exactly, are Dublin and I going to get over the hedge?

Chapter 8
Singer

A rope could pull me up the tree—if only we could find enough strong vines to make the rope.

A knife could, maybe, cut through the hedge—if only we could make something with a razor edge.

A fire could burn down the hedge—if only we could, well, start a fire.

One by one, our ideas collapse. I am starting to hate the sight of this bramble wall rising stubbornly in our path. I'm not sure why I ever thought it was pretty. While my frustration spikes, Jaxon just seems distracted. I'm sure his mind is with Joy, trying to envision whatever she might be facing on her own and hoping with every heartbeat that she's okay.

The only other thing I can think of is digging. I sit near the hedge, scraping half-heartedly at the packed dirt. Dublin paws at the ground next to me, but even his rugged claws don't make much of an impression. And anyway, digging takes more energy than I can possibly muster. It's not just the exhaustion, which is ever-present and makes my muscles feel like tissue paper. It's worse: the thirst is back. I'm dreaming of water again, of rivers and rain and pools and puddles. But this time there's nothing to quench the craving.

Jaxon is the one who finally points out that since we can't go over, through or under the hedge, our only other option is to go around it.

I'm not sure that's going to be possible. There's a good chance the hedge runs across the TimeTilter with no gaps. On the other hand, I don't have a better idea.

When I first stepped into the TimeTilter, everything around me was so unfamiliar, so strange and spectacular at the same time. Part of what kept me moving was wanting to see the next vivid color and distorted terrain. This time, as Jaxon and I start moving again, I don't care what our surroundings look like. Since we're moving along the hedge, it's not that exciting anyway; just brambles and more brambles, still draped with strands of cobweb. So I keep my head down and concentrate on taking my next steps. I try to spare Dublin by not leaning on him too much. He looks tired and ragged too. His fur, which used to be so glossy, is tangled and matted with dirt and little twigs.

"Sorry I got you into this, buddy," I tell him. I know Dublin well enough to interpret the look he gives me: even after everything we've been through, he'd rather be here with me than anywhere else. I ruffle his ears and add, "I wish we were both anywhere else."

Jaxon looks over his shoulder at me. "Are you talking to your dog?"

"Uh, yes," I say, bristling a bit. "Unless you have some better conversation to offer."

Jaxon gives me what could almost be called a smile. "I might. With all due respect to a creature named after the great city of Dublin, who no doubt has tremendously interesting things to say."

I play along. "Dublin, we'll have to get back to our discussion later. Jaxon wants to speak now."

"I just thought," Jaxon says mildly, "that maybe we could ask Dram how he got past the hedge with Delia and Royaltee. And if there's anything to drink around here other than poisoned water."

It's worth a try.

I pull out my leaf and start a message. It's short and really not much more than a pile of questions. There's more I want to say. Like how unbearably guilty I feel that Jaxon is here with me. How hopeless I feel about getting out of here. How scared I am that something bad is going to happen to Joy. And how much I wish Dram were here in this same space, in my perception, so I could see the person who I think would understand each thing I'm feeling. But with Jaxon close by, those things go unsaid.

We keep moving as artificial day turns to artificial dusk, making our way slowly and silently along the hedge that never seems to end.

Chapter 9
Singer

When Dram's answer comes, the first think I want to do is break my promise to Jaxon and not share.

I slow down to let Jaxon get further ahead and even start to record a reply to Dram before good sense takes over. I can't keep this a secret. The message must have appeared on Jaxon's leaf too; he just hasn't noticed it yet. At my call, Jaxon slows his pace to mine and we look together.

Dram: Singer, I am here. We got past the hedge.

Royaltee found a way. She saw a place where the branches looked different. Well, they looked different to her though not to Delia or me. Different on the inside, she said. I don't know what she meant but she was right. At this one place, the branches bent like rubber. All we had to do was pull them apart and step through. But that's no help to you. We are well away from that hedge and there's no way to tell you where we came through.

So Dram is nowhere near us, I think. My chest squeezes in and I take a few deep breaths to push back the disappointment. I write back as quickly as I can. And Dram answers again—as fast as a text message on my phone. Heart thumping, with Jaxon wide-eyed by my side, I have my first real conversation with Dram.

Me: I don't even know where to start. I'm so relieved you're there and that you answered. And Royaltee is still with you—that's good. If she can see inside branches, she must have something weird going on with her sight, just like you and me and Jaxon. What about Delia—is she okay?

Dram: Yes. Very tired, like all of us. And angry, which I think helps make her strong.

Me: What is she angry about? Besides the obvious—that we're all stuck in here.

Dram: Nothing you could guess. She's mad because she doesn't have anything to draw with—no spray paint cans or markers in here. She keeps saying that she sees purple everywhere and she wants to draw it so she can remember how beautiful it is.

        Sorry, I had to wait a minute for her to move away. Now I can tell you that I'm looking all around and purple is *not* everywhere. But I don't think Del is making this up. She is seeing something I don't see.

Me: We're all seeing things that nobody else can. There's my night-sight and Jaxon's far-sight. You can look into the past and Royaltee can look inside things. We've all had our vision messed with.

Dram: Yes. I've thought about that. We've had our vision changed. But not in bad ways. More like—in ways that help us survive in here.

Me: I think that freaks me out more than anything else about being in here. It's like we're being experimented on. It makes me want to get out of here even faster.

Dram: Really? I think it's not so bad. Better than anyplace Delia and I have been for a while. I think we'll stop by this stream and rest and have a drink—

Me: Don't! I told you, any water you find will be packed with superzeitgeber. Trust me, drinking any of that is *much* worse than being thirsty. And you really think this place is *not so bad*? We're trapped in here with those horrible shadows and—

Dram: If you could see me now, you would know I'm joking. Sorry. Del says I'm not very good at that.

        I wish I could see you. And hear you. So much technology and no video? No audio? These messages are something but not enough. Though your words are music I could sing to.

Me: If you could see *me* now, you'd know I'm smiling. Thanks for that. Of course we're also annoying Jaxon. He says we're wasting time but—

Dram: He's right. I would like your smile to stay but there's something else I have to say. It's important. I've had another memory. Another vision from the past. I don't remember seeing it before but I know it's real.

(Del, yes, I trust her. I do. Shhhh, enough now.)

This vision is from right after I got into the TimeTilter. Right after getting that big dose of superzeitgeber. I looked back at the room, the one with all the arched glass windows—do you remember? I think that's where you started too. For just a second, the glass was still transparent. I could see Angelie through the windows and she looked right at me but I could tell *she couldn't see me*. Then everything in my sight started shaking back and forth and I had to close my eyes. When I opened them again she was gone.

Singer.

Are you still there?

Me: Yes, I'm here. Jaxon and I were just...trying to understand. Are you saying that Angelie can't see us in here?

Dram: I think so. Yes. All this time I thought she would know exactly where we are. But now, after having this vision? I'm not so sure.

Me: I never thought about it before. But...if we can't see each other when we're on different time perceptions...then I guess it makes sense that Angelie can't see us either. I remember what she said to us: That we should stay together. That if we go down different perception paths, we won't be able to see each other. The thing I don't get is *why*. Why would she put us in the TimeTilter if she can't even see what we're doing?

Dram: I don't know. But that makes me think of something Royaltee said to me. She said: why are we in such a hurry to get out of here? Maybe that's when things will get worse.

Singer? Have I lost you? I didn't mean to scare you away.

What happened? Where are you? Talk to me as soon as you can. I need to know you're okay.

Singer, are you there?

I know Dram is sending more messages and everything he has written is rocking wildly in my brain but there's no time to answer.

Something is wrong with Jaxon. Something big.

He stands ten feet away from me—how did he get over there?—with his eyes unfocused and his arms stretched out in front of him like he's reaching for something. I drop my leaf and run to him.

This close to Jaxon I can see his lips moving. I lean in to hear him say, over and over, "Where am I?"

I grab Jaxon's arm and shake him and shout but I might as well not be there. I can't break him loose from whatever is holding him.

Right in this moment I am completely sure that whether we stay in the TimeTilter or get out—either way, it will end badly.

Chapter 10
Jaxon

It was back but worse than before.

Jaxon was seeing things again, things that weren't really there, as if he were looking through someone else's eyes.

Fractured impressions of dark and light.

A marsh.

Shadows. Too many shadows.

A door made of dull corrugated metal. Closed. Then open.

A room. No time to see what was in it. A struggle. He was pushed and pulled. The walls and the floor swirled and tipped. The ceiling hovered overhead as if he'd fallen on his back. A face loomed and disappeared.

Then dark.

Then nothingness.

For way too long, nothingness.

The colors, when they came, made him want to shield his eyes. Too bright. Too surreal. The marsh. The bridge. The rise of woods.

Where they had started.

Back at the beginning.

Chapter 11
Singer

There is one moment, while Jaxon is still gripped by his vision, when I nearly fall apart.

The light from the sky has faded, spilling us into nighttime, which matches my mood: I feel like I'm at the bottom of a deep, dark well that's collapsing inward bit by bit.

I sit on the ground with my arms wrapped around Dublin's neck and cry without tears.

Then Jaxon breaks free from his vision or trance or whatever it is, still looking dazed. He kneels down beside me and tells me everything he saw. With a hitch in his voice, Jaxon ends with this bombshell: everything he described—the door, the struggle, even the nothingness—wasn't happening to him. He's sure it was happening to Joy.

He was seeing it all through her eyes.

I feel like giving Jaxon one more shake, as if that will help his words make sense to me. "Why do you even think that?"

Jaxon looks down, his voice low. "It's not the first time I've done this. A few times before, while Joy was still here, I just...hacked her vision. I didn't mean to." He exhales heavily. "I can't even control it."

I slide away from Jaxon, but not because I'm scared or don't believe him. It's just so I have room to think. Dublin moves with me and, for the first time since we entered the TimeTilter, he whines. It's a soft sound, barely audible, and usually reserved for times when my stress levels spike.

But something different is going on inside me now. I remember how one time—what seems like a very long time ago—I went with my parents and the goldens to Vermont for a climbing competition. We passed a construction site that was mostly hidden by a mesh fence. Towering high above the fence, impossible to miss, was a crane—one of those self-erecting cranes that builds itself upward until it's so tall you can't even imagine being at the top without feeling dizzy. That's what my thoughts feel like right now, like they're building and unfolding into something big enough to take us somewhere.

"Jaxon," I say calmly, "you didn't do it. You didn't hack Joy's vision."

"What?" Jaxon blinks.

"You said you can't control it," I say. "That's what made me realize—it's *her* power, not yours."

The look on Jaxon's face says that this is a one-hundred-and-eighty-degree turnaround for him, this idea that he didn't do anything wrong. That Joy might still be reaching out to him after all.

"Tell me again," I say. "Tell me everything you saw."

It's obvious to me that Joy, whether she meant to or not, sent us a message. She gave us information and it's up to us to make sense of it. We need to figure out what happened to her.

In the darkness, Jaxon can barely see me, but for now it doesn't matter. We're not going anywhere; we just need to talk this through. Together Jaxon and I start pulling at the strands of his vision, a clenched knot that slowly unravels to let us get at the truth of it.

First, the marsh and the shadows. If our theory about the shadows being some sort of border patrol is right, then Joy must have reached an outer wall. And then she found a door—a way out. All that information seems to mean that she really made it to the West Portal out of the TimeTilter. Which has been our destination this whole time. That's what Angelie said we had to do in order to get out of here. That was supposed to be the end of the ride.

But something went wrong. Joy must have seen something she didn't like, something suspicious. She kicked and punched and struggled.

"That's Joy, for sure," Jaxon says. "She gave them a fight."

I think of Joy, facing some terrible unknown completely on her own, and I wonder if I could have summoned up the same boldness and backbone. As tired and rejected as she must have felt, it couldn't have been easy to resist.

Jaxon sums up the rest of the vision: an unfamiliar face, then darkness. Joy lost the fight—and got dumped right back into the TimeTilter.

"*Why?*" My shout comes out of nowhere. The word catapults out of my throat and soars into the air before settling around me like a heavy cloak. I want to shake it off but it's the one word that won't go away and doesn't seem to have any answers. Why is this happening to me? Why did Angelie have to choose me—or any of us—for this exhausting, endless game? Why are we in here? And why should we even try to get out if someone is just going to throw us back in?

The fear and hopelessness that are never far under the surface come rising back up like water in a clogged drain. I scramble to my hands and knees. With Dublin beside me, I crawl around Jaxon in a sudden and frantic search for my leaf. I threw it aside when Jaxon first got caught up in his vision. Dimly I hear Jaxon calling my name but I can't stop hunting. Just like Jaxon can see through Joy's eyes, I feel like I can see Dram's world through his words. Not just his present world, here in the TimeTilter, but his past and his guilt and his fears. All so similar to my own. That connection we have—I can't lose it. Not now.

"Singer! Stop! It's okay," Jaxon says.

It's his turn, this time, to bring me back to the here and now. He reaches for me, relying on touch to find my arm, and pulls me to my feet.

"You don't need your leaf. I still have mine." He offers the leaf to me on the palm of his hand and I take it gently.

With a quick exhale I see that there's a new message.

Dram: I don't know if I'll hear from you again. But I'm thinking about something you told me. What Angelie said before she sent you into the TimeTilter. That someone wants us to stay in here, but we should never stop trying to get out. So don't stop trying, Singer. Please don't stop.

I send a reply to Dram with shaky fingers.

Then another.

And another.

TimeTilter seconds gather into minutes that grow like a ball of string. Nothing comes back.

When there's no more point to waiting, I sigh and square my shoulders.

"Okay," I say. "Let's go. Time to move on."

Jaxon pauses and I swivel to face him.

"I've got this night vision thing, remember?" I say. "I can find a trail."

"It's not that," he says hesitantly. "Just a thought. Like Dram said, Angelie tried to give us a warning. At the time I figured she was playing some sort of mind game. But now I wonder...what if she wasn't? What if she was really trying to save us from...something else?"

Seconds slip by. I can't think of anything Angelie has done that would make me believe she's on our side. Except for that warning. *Never stop looking for a way out.* If we had listened to Angelie, then maybe Joy wouldn't have headed straight to the West Portal—and right back into the TimeTilter.

And there is one other thing: the unfamiliar face, seen by Jaxon through Joy's eyes. So it wasn't Angelie who put Joy back in here. It was someone else.

"I think," I say to Jaxon, "that we need to find a different way out."

Chapter 12
Monet

Monet was having no luck finding a way in.

Her ID card still wasn't working at any entrance into the TimeTilter. No surprise there. With a smooth audacity that Monet had never realized she possessed, she managed to swipe an ID tag off a security officer's desk. She tried it at three different doors before scurrying back to return the tag exactly as she'd found it, but the whole maneuver ended up being pointless. It looked like the TimeTilter was closed even to the security department.

What was going on in there?

Keeping her head down and taking a back staircase instead of the elevator, Monet returned to her own office. Though she'd been gone no more than thirty minutes, she half expected to find the room as dark and deserted as Hunter's office. But everything was still in place. Monet pulled her company-issued laptop back out of her bag and opened it up. The familiar Collusia logo pulsed on the start-up screen. Monet stared at it for five seconds and then slammed the laptop shut.

This time, when she walked out of the building, Monet brought her phone but left the computer behind. She found her car—an easy-to-spot red hybrid—in a nearly empty parking lot. Monet slunk low in the seat, turned on her phone and opened a browser. Time for a new approach: a digital hunt for data.

Monet had never had much interest in Collusia's history. What she knew about the company before she was hired wasn't much: just that Collusia was a gigantic company that conducted research in bioengineering, sustainability and construction. That they had a good record of philanthropy and community outreach. And, of course, that they were developing the TimeTilter. After joining the company, Monet was always too hyped up and overwhelmed with her new job to pay attention to any projects in other departments.

You're never afraid to take risks. You just jump into things without knowing if they're going to turn out great or not. Monet had heard those admiring words from her sister a million times. She'd done the same thing with this job: jumped in without knowing what she was really heading into.

Well, that was about to change. Monet scrolled through her search results. The top hits were mostly self-congratulatory press releases by Collusia describing the company's latest research initiatives. There were a lot of articles about the upcoming opening of the TimeTilter. Those were more interesting and Monet did a speed-read of each one. It was nice to see herself quoted as the lead environmental designer. But there wasn't, as Monet had impossibly hoped, any breaking news about nonfunctioning ID cards.

Monet refocused her search on Dr. Angelie Bonneville. Nothing new there, either. The dozens of articles she skimmed all mentioned Angelie only to credit her as the Collusia mastermind who developed the superzeitgeber. It was as if Angelie had no other identity on the Internet. Well, to be fair, that was a pretty defining accomplishment. But it wasn't helping Monet dig any deeper.

Monet closed her eyes and took a breath. How to narrow the search when she didn't even know what she was looking for? And speaking of looking for something, where on earth was Hunter? If only he were here to help her. From the cramped seat of her car in the far corner of the remote parking lot, Monet's mind flashed on the vacant interior of Hunter's office. And then on the whiteboard with the smeared and faded marker swipes.

Yes.

She sprang upright and typed "angelie bonneville starfish" into the browser's search bar.

One hit. Monet clicked the link.

Alarming Starfish Dries Up

Gamers lament! Alarming Starfish (Al-Star) Studios avoided bankruptcy this month by selling out to goliath Collusia Corporation. Al-Star is the creator of some of the most obscure but fan-honored first-person online games, such as the genre-defying Dog Party and the nothing-less-than-alarming Red House of Horror.

Fans will be disappointed to hear that Al-Star's Angelie Bonneville, engineer and programmer extraordinaire, has accepted a position at Collusia. That spells an end to the innovative games and free expansions that won Al-Star such a faithful band of followers.

An inside source, who asked for anonymity in order to speak candidly, reports that Al-Star had sunk a massive amount of funds into a new Bonneville invention: the superzeitgeber, a chemical inhaled by users that can alter their perception of time. Sounds fishy to us, but our source claims it's the real deal. A problem with the superzeitgeber, in the form of unexpected long-term side effects, is what reportedly caused Al-Star to go belly up.

That was it. Monet frowned. This story was old—the buyout had happened years ago. But the URL...she recognized it as an obscure but definitely reputable news source, despite the breezy writing style.

So. If this article could be believed, she'd made a few important connections. First of all, it looked like Angelie Bonneville had come up with the superzeitgeber while she was an employee of Alarming Starfish Studios—something Hunter must have figured out. After Collusia bought out Alarming Starfish, the company must have taken over the rights to the superzeitgeber technology. Maybe that's why Angelie made the move to Collusia, so she could keep working on her research.

The bigger revelation was the problem with the superzeitgeber. Monet had never once heard any mention of long-term side effects. Had the issue been fixed? Or had Collusia managed to purge and suppress any other mention of it the media?

With the TimeTilter shut down and inaccessible, Monet had a feeling the superzeitgeber problem was still very much in play.

Chapter 13
Dram

Singer. You are there.

I was very relieved to see your message.

(Del, stop nudging me. What is your problem?)

(Oh.)

Okay, Singer, to be honest those words don't begin to cover how I feel. When I didn't hear from you I hated the TimeTilter more completely than I've ever hated anything because I thought it had somehow conquered you. I should have known better.

(Dellie Bellie, can you go find me some moss? No it doesn't have to be purple. Any color is okay. I think I see some way over there. Yes, it's okay, I can still see you.)

Now I have a lot more to say. The first thing I've been thinking about was what Angelie told you: that someone wants to keep us *in* the TimeTilter. Why would that be? I think we are here to test something. Not the game, but something more serious. More dangerous. And we were chosen for this test because we're all alone in some way. No one is likely to notice, at least not right away, if we disappear.

Everything you told me about Joy—and the vision she sent to Jaxon— adds up to one thing in my head. It has to be the superzeitgeber.

Here's how I think it was supposed to happen: We get prepped with the superzeitgeber. We travel across the TimeTilter, coming out the West Portal as we've been told. Angelie—or someone else who is telling her what to do—checks to see if our minds still work like they should, and if we can handle the return to normal time perception. Then we're treated with a higher dose of superzeitgeber and sent back into the TimeTilter. Do you see where this is heading? They can just keep taking us out and throwing us back in. For as long as we can survive it. And then they'll know the limits of the superzeitgeber. They'll know what works and what can go wrong. And if any of us doesn't make it? It doesn't matter. I don't think they ever meant to let us go.

You will get now why I didn't want Delia to hear this.

When Joy shared her sight with Jaxon, she saved all of our lives. Because now, like you said, we know we have to find another way out.

I don't know how that will happen. But I do know this: We each might have been alone on the outside. But in here, Singer, we are all together.

Chapter 14
Singer

When I see Dram's words—*here, Singer, we are all together*—I know right away exactly what has to happen.

In order to find a way out of the TimeTilter, we really do all need to be together. In the same place. In the same time perception.

I've asked Dram, Delia and Royaltee to turn around and come back through the hedge as soon as there's enough light. Royaltee will do her part: she'll try to locate more branches that bend like rubber so that they can step through. Then we'll all be on the same side of the hedge—which will be great, except for the fact that it stretches across the TimeTilter. It's a very long stretch. What are the chances of us running into each other accidentally? I have a feeling that particular number involves a lot of zeros to the right of the decimal point.

We'll need to narrow down the search.

Jaxon peers up at the fake sun that is finally making an appearance, giving us a better look around. "You know..." Jaxon starts and pauses. I wave my hands in a "keep going" roll. "We were heading to the West Portal when this hedge stopped us. And we've been keeping the hedge to our left while we try to get around it. So, I think that means we're heading...north?"

I nod. He's right. We must be pretty close to the north wall of the TimeTilter. "So if they walk in the same direction," I chime in, "eventually they should run into us. Assuming that they aren't already ahead of us." Okay, so the plan isn't perfect, but it's starting to increase the odds. And I'm starting to feel, just a bit, like a balloon bobbing on ocean waves: there's a sort of bright lightness in me that could be tossed either toward the shore or back out to sea at any moment. For now, I'm hanging on to my giddy mood. When Jaxon starts gathering rocks, branches, moss, leaves—anything that's loose on the ground—into a big pile, I'm so busy envisioning us all together that it barely registers. I stand and smile at him without either helping or asking what he's doing.

"Um...Singer?"

I tilt my head at him. "What? Enough olagonin' and standin' around like a muppet?"

Jaxon shakes his head at me and points to his messy pyramid of forest debris. "They could walk right by and never see us. You have to help me build some kind of signal that they can't miss."

It's true. We won't be able to perceive Dram and his team, so we need to guide them close, to guarantee that we bump into each other and make the connection that will pull us all into the same perception path. I take a more critical look at Jaxon's structure. Even though it doesn't look like anything I've ever seen before, the problem is that nothing around here does. Uniqueness doesn't really stand out in the TimeTilter. No matter how carefully I describe this "signal" to Dram, I still think he could easily pass it by.

I turn to Jaxon, who has stepped back to watch. He's silhouetted against the hedge. The artificial sun, rising higher, casts rays of light that dance around the lacy cobwebs. I'm struck again by how beautiful the cobwebs are. I remember something else. The silk that those orb-weaver spiders use to make the web—it reflects ultraviolet light. That's a good thing for spiders: insects can see ultraviolet light, so they're attracted to the web.

"Jaxon," I say unsteadily, "*insects can see ultraviolet light.*"

He shakes his head again. "Where are we heading with this?"

"If humans could see ultraviolet light, it would look like a purple glow." I wait for Jaxon to get it. He needs more. "*Purple.* Like the purple that Delia sees everywhere. She can see ultraviolet light reflecting off the cobwebs."

Understanding dawns on Jaxon's face.

He whirls around and starts to pull cobwebs off the hedge. The brambles nip and scratch his hands but that doesn't slow him down. While I quickly send Dram a message telling him what we're doing, Jaxon drapes the silky, sticky strands over himself, over me, over a puzzled but unresisting Dublin.

Soon we're covered in thick layers. We settle ourselves next to Jaxon's forest pile. While Delia won't be able to see us directly, she shouldn't miss these three weird bulky patches of purple.

It could be a long wait until they find us. They could still walk right by us.

But I feel my balloon of hopefulness bobbing steadily closer to shore.

Chapter 15
Singer

Whon you're thirsty, it's pure torment to be offered water that you can't drink.

As we sit and wait in our cobweb robes, I watch beads of dew gather and slide between the layers of web. I want to cup the moisture in my hand and lap it up. But I can't do that. I won't go through another descent into superzeitgeber overload.

So we wait.

And we watch.

And the water droplets converge into untouchable, taunting pools at our feet.

It's hot in here. The source of light, or SOL—which is what I've started calling the TimeTilter's sun—slowly changes position overhead in an arc that mimics the path of the real sun.

All the while we are counting on Delia, a seven-year-old kid, to notice three purple shapes that are invisible to other human eyes. The longer we sit, the less probable that seems.

Until Dublin barks.

It's his people bark, the one he uses when he sees someone and wants attention. Short, firm and friendly. His tail is wagging like a flag caught in a windstorm.

There's the lightest touch on my cheek, a tentative sweep of fingertips.

In the time it takes to blink, everything changes.

They are here.

I see Delia first, right in front of me. She rolls the cobwebs down off my shoulders and stares up at me with round eyes in an elfin face.

"You're Singer," she says, with so much soft hopefulness in her voice that I want to hug her. But before I can do that she spins away and rushes to Dublin, wrapping her arms completely around him. She meets him forehead to forehead and he licks her chin and they are both completely and happily absorbed.

Which lets me turn my attention...to Dram. To black hair swept sideways above two dark, kind eyes. He's been watching his sister but now he looks at me as I swipe the rest of the cobwebs off my clothes. When I'm done he still hasn't moved, and I know right away that he's a bit afraid to say anything because that's exactly how I feel, as if there aren't any words that can exactly convey what we're going through in this moment. I step forward, and he steps forward, and we give each other hesitant half smiles. Then I can't wait another second for either of us to speak, because who needs words anyway, and I leap forward to give him a hug.

I can't think of anything else right now, not where we are or where we're going or how we'll get out of the TimeTilter.

Because he's here, really here. Rock-steady and real.

Sonia Ellis

PART III

COLLUSION:

a secret conspiracy formed with
the intent to deceive

Sonia Ellis

Chapter 1
Royaltee

It was Royaltee's chance to speak, to say things both astonishing and true, but the words wouldn't come.

When Singer, Jaxon and the red-gold dog materialized in front of Delia, Royaltee stood back. She watched as Delia buried herself in the comfort of the dog's soft fur. She watched as Singer and Dram gazed at each other with painful sweetness. She watched as Jaxon stood, head down, aching for Joy to appear.

They all knew she was here. Eventually, Singer and Jaxon turned to her and gave her a welcome that was amiable but awkward—the only balance possible between people who had been complete strangers until now, but from this moment on would rely on each other for everything.

After that was done, everyone's attention slipped away from Royaltee. She was used to this. Her still face, the thin sweep of her hair, her faraway eyes—all these things gave them nothing to hold on to. She might as well have faded back into another perception path.

So she watched as the four of them bunched together. She watched as thoughts and gestures were tossed out, caught, discarded and finally gathered into a plan. They wanted to force their way out. They would make some sort of battering ram that could smash through a door along an outer wall. There would be a wooden frame for carrying the ram and vines for binding the pieces together.

"It won't work," Royaltee said. "The pieces you're gathering—I can see inside them all. How they'll bend or stretch or break. It won't work."

No one turned to look at her.

No one heard a thing.

Which made sense because Royaltee's lips never moved and the words never left her head.

It wasn't just that the materials were wrong. The hope was wrong. And useless. What was the point of trying to escape the TimeTilter...when they would only be thrown back inside again? Royaltee knew this. She knew it sharply and personally: it had happened to her. The first time she, like Joy, had found her solo way to the West Portal. Only to be prepped again with a higher dose of superzeitgeber and sent back in. Pathetically hopeful, she had forged a new trail across the TimeTilter, back to the exit point. And here she was yet again, this time teamed with Dram and Delia in a hopeless cyclic journey.

Why didn't she speak and tell them everything?

Was she really such a coward?

Yes.

There was too much at stake. Royaltee had no doubt about the consequences. If she told the truth right now...the truth about that horrible person who found her and forced her into the TimeTilter; the truth about Royaltee's connection—no, that was too weak a word—her *bond* with Angelie; the truth about the threats that kept both of them silent and compliant...no, she couldn't even think it. It wasn't an option. Dram, Singer and Jaxon—they would understand why she didn't speak. They wouldn't have either, in her place. Singer was here because she would never abandon the red-gold dog. Jaxon had led Joy into this world because he wanted to set her free, though Joy didn't see that yet. Dram—this Royaltee had seen for herself—had no greater desire than to keep Delia safe. They all knew what it meant to protect someone you love. They would understand why she stared and said nothing.

It took some moments for Royaltee to realize that the view in front of her had changed.

The hedge—the whole brambly, cobwebbed length of it—was gone.

Dram, Delia, Singer, Jaxon...all gone.

The gusts of motion as they gathered and built and argued...all faded into quiet.

The landscape morphed abruptly and completely into a thick forest of trees so tall that she couldn't see their tops. The trees began to rotate around her with a stately grace. She felt as if she were spinning in a slow circle as she stared up the sky.

She was alone in the stillness. On her own in this perception. All she could do was look up, up, up at—

"Royaltee!"

It was Jaxon, calling her back. Royaltee blinked as the odd vision dropped from sight, dumping her as decisively as a slammed door.

"I know that look," Jaxon said. He leaned in close and put a hand on her shoulder. "I've been through that too. What did you see?"

Royaltee paused. She was faintly surprised to be noticed, much less spoken to.

"I'm not sure," she said slowly. "I was in a forest. And I was looking up, high into the trees. But it felt like I was..."

"Seeing through someone else's eyes?" Jaxon finished for her.

Royaltee nodded, not trusting her voice to adequately describe all that she'd seen.

Jaxon's face nearly glowed, as if Royaltee had given him an unexpected but utterly perfect gift. "It's Joy," he said. "It has to be. She's the only one of us who can share her sight."

Royaltee did not understand how such a skill could be possible. It made as little sense as her own ability to see, when she chose to, the tiny inner structure of things. But she had come to accept that as real. So seeing through someone else's eyes...why not? It was, really, no more or less extraordinary.

"I should have known," Jaxon said. He nearly bounced on his toes, buoyed by what he seemed to regard as proof that Joy was okay. "She's fighting back. She's trying to send us a message. Royaltee, please, tell me *everything* you remember. Please, think."

"Just trees," Royaltee murmured. "I don't see how that can help us. If it was Joy, then she was in a forest with very tall trees, and she was looking up, and spinning in a circle maybe, but always looking up." She peered more closely at Jaxon. His face had drained, as pale now as it had been bright before. "What is it?

He sighed. "I was just remembering...something sad. When Joy climbed a tree to get over the hedge. That was when I lost her. When I let her go."

Royaltee nodded again, giving him a gentle nudge to go on.

"She was perched up there," Jaxon continued, "so strong and sure of herself. And one of the last things she said was...*I can see things a lot more clearly from up here.*" Jaxon took a deep breath. "I wish we had that now. A way to see things clearly."

Royaltee laughed out loud.

When Jaxon looked at her, pained and startled at her weird reaction, she only laughed harder.

"Jaxon," she said. "You're right. She did send us a message." She reeled her laughter in and tilted her head. "Don't you hear it? She's telling us: look up. The way out. It's *up*."

Jaxon lifted his gaze automatically to the sky.

Things moved quickly after that. Jaxon squeezed Royaltee tight, breathless with gratitude and excitement, and dashed off to tell everyone what she had seen. The battering ram was discarded. The new plan: find a way to climb high, all the way to the sky.

As Royaltee moved to join them, she saw Jaxon cast quick glances at her. She knew what he was thinking. Why Royaltee? Why had Joy sent the vision to her and not to him?

To Royaltee the answer was simple, though she would never share it with Jaxon. When Joy sent her sight out into the TimeTilter, Royaltee's mind had been the only one open to listening.

Chapter 2
Dram

Is anybody out there?

We're all together now. Royaltee, Delia and I are with Singer and Jaxon—and of course Dublin, who it's hard to think of separately from Singer.

But Joy, you're on your own. Maybe you will see this message. Maybe there is someone else lost in this place. Or maybe no one will ever read this. But just in case, I'm going to record it all, exactly as it happened: how we found a way to get out.

We went up. That's what you should know first. Up, hoping we could reach the artificial sky. Up, hoping to rise above the mist that keeps our minds time-tilted. We didn't know how long much longer we could survive under the influence of the superzeitgeber. But we were all scared, too, because we didn't know what would happen when we left it behind.

One thing, at least, we knew. We were all on a path that Angelie couldn't see. So she wouldn't try to stop us.

We started with a tree. The tallest one we could find, with a solid trunk and sturdy branches that pointed sideways like outstretched arms.

Have you found the yellow fungus that grows at the base of many trees near the hedge? Jaxon says they look like stacks of pancakes. That is true, but they bend less and hold more weight than a pancake ever could. Jaxon and Singer showed us what to do next. Each slice of fungus has a hooked stem. We hitched those stems into pieces of bark on the tree trunk. The fungus became steps up the tree.

Then I made a ladder with branches and vines. This was not difficult. I will tell you how you can do it yourself.
1. Gather two long lengths of strong vine.
2. Find ten short branches, each about one foot long. Search for branches that will not break under your weight.
3. Lay the branches out on the ground, spaced as far apart as the steps on a ladder.
4. Run the vines along the left and right sides of the ladder.
5. Knot the vines around each branch. A constriction knot is good, but if you don't know what that is, just be sure your knots are tight.

Royaltee and Jaxon used the steps to reach the first branch that was ten feet from the ground. They tied the top of my ladder to the branch. Singer couldn't climb the steps but somehow she climbed that ladder with Delia right behind her to give her a boost and balance whenever she needed it.

If anyone who is reading this knows Singer at all, you would say: *this doesn't make sense. Singer wouldn't go up the ladder without Dublin. She wouldn't leave him behind.* That is true. So you will not be surprised to hear that we had to find a way to get Dublin up the tree too. We made a sling from my tattered jacket. When Singer positioned the sling under Dublin, he stood still and gave her nothing but trust. We attached vines to the sling and when we were all in the first branch—I climbed up after Singer and Delia—we pulled him up too, all of us together.

That is an image that I will remember, for the unlikely humor of it: his feathery legs and huge paws dangling over the edges of the sling and his body swinging gently as we tugged him up as smoothly as we could.

Then we were on our way. We did the same thing all over again, to the next branch and the next after that. We each had our moment of faltering. I saw that Singer grew more and more tired, her worn out legs giving way more and more often. I saw that Jaxon could hardly bear to leave the ground, always hoping for Joy to appear out of nowhere. I saw Royaltee look up at the height of the tree with growing doubt. And I felt the bite of fear in the way Delia's hands clutched at my arm.

As for myself, I kept my attention on Singer, ready to move fast if she needed me. She was so tired, with an exhaustion beyond what I have ever felt or seen. Each time she pulled herself higher up the ladder, she drew a powerful breath and her eyes turned bright as fire. Her movements were a song, the kind of song that you can't shake loose. But as weary as she was, she didn't lose her courage, and that kept me in possession of my own.

At one point, as I struggled up to Singer's side, I drew on that courage to tell her, "I'm taking a picture of you in my head so that I won't forget this moment. So that when we get out of here, I can remind you of how strong you are. That is a memory I intend to hold on to."

I thought I had said the wrong thing and should have kept silent, because Singer's face held some emotion that looked too much like sadness. Then she smiled and took my hand and held it, just for a second, against her cheek.

We climbed on, one hundred percent on hope.

We didn't know what would happen when we got to the top of the tree. Jaxon, whose power of sight was as keen as an eagle's, was hoping he would be able to spot something hanging from the "sky" ceiling—any sort of hook or beam that we could toss a vine around to haul ourselves up. Royallee analyzed the branches, the bark, even the leaves, all the materials we had around us, thinking that maybe we could build on to the top of the tree, making it rise higher and higher.

What happened, instead, was something we should have expected in this place of skewed perceptions but never did.

In the end, when we reached the treetop, we didn't have to climb any further. From here, where we perched on a high shaky branch, the sky was suddenly in easy reach of our fingertips.

All along, the extreme and far-flung height of the distant blue sky and wandering clouds had been nothing more than an illusion.

Chapter 3
Singer

When Dram says he wants to take a picture of me and keep it forever, my heart floods and I can't breathe.

The world of the TimeTilter pales around me. Without knowing it, Dram has tapped into a memory that I've never been able to shake.

It starts with a party.

My friend Callie turned eleven a month after I did. The differences between how our birthdays were marked—that was something I was used to. Mine passed with a small cake after dinner and a neat arrangement of presents next to my plate. Afterwards the wrapping paper was folded away for reuse and then it was over; I was left alone to read my new books and try on my new sweater.

Callie's birthday party was a messy explosion: busted piñatas, popping balloons, kids stomping up and down the stairs, and wrapping paper torn to confetti-sized bits that could never be reused. All that was punctuated with the flash of Mrs. Kent's camera. She grabbed everyone she could catch hold of and marched them into shoulder-to-shoulder poses.

When the party was over, I stayed. I was still Callie's best friend, and Callie got what she asked for: a sleepover with me, a late-night movie and sweet caramel-covered popcorn. Callie had a bunk bed in her room and was always nice about letting me have the upper bunk, the one that was closer to the neon stars glued to her ceiling in the outlines of horses and space ships. After the movie, Mrs. Kent took a few more photos of Callie and me as we stuffed popcorn into our mouths and lounged on the living room sofa, making silly faces.

Finally, laughing and giving up, Mrs. Kent handed the camera to me. "Here, want to try?" she asked.

I did. I arranged Callie and her brother Liam on the cushions and posed Mrs. Kent and Mr. Kent behind them. Then I took picture after picture, trying different angles and telling ridiculous jokes to get serious Liam to smile. It felt right, a moment of being one of the family, the one who could be counted on to take a good picture when no one else could.

I didn't get back to Callie's house for a week because I had a tough line-up of doctor appointments and physical therapy on my leg—part of a treatment that wasn't going too well. The next Saturday, I settled back into Callie's house for the day, looking forward to retelling stories from the party. It wasn't until after lunch that I wandered into the living room and saw the latest photos that Mrs. Kent had hung on the wall.

There was Callie in a cardboard party hat, one hand poised over her cake, with her parents and Liam circled around her. Next to that was a photo of Callie holding up a ukulele that she had been begging for, her eyes wide and her mouth in a comical O. There was a group picture that must have been taken before I arrived. I wasn't in any of the photos. And these weren't the pictures I had taken with such care and pride. There was no sign I had even been in the house on the night of Callie's birthday party. I knew what all these photos meant to the Kent family: every one reinforced how completely they belonged together, loved one another, here in this space that was their home. Every one was a framed reminder from Mr. and Mrs. Kent to Callie and Liam that they were treasured, even in their messiest moments. But I had no place on their walls. I didn't hold enough value for my life to be recorded here.

I spent the rest of the afternoon with Callie because I had to. After that day, I kept making excuses not to go over to her house. Callie got impatient with inviting me over only to be refused. Our friendship faltered and finally faded.

From that time on, I saw myself as a discarded photograph, corners curling in, the image fading to blankness.

So when Dram says I'm a memory he intends to hold on to, he has no way of knowing that he has said exactly the right thing.

Chapter 4
Singer

Up close, it's hard to understand how we ever believed that the sky looked real.

From this angle, where I can reach out with my fingertips and touch it, I see that the sky is constructed out of some huge number of individual interlocking panels. Each panel is a few feet across and looks like a shiny TV screen. In fact, I guess that's sort of what the panels are: pieces of a vast, continuous animation of sky. As I watch, the foamy edge of a pale pink cloud slides into view. From the ground, the panels all merge together. But from here I can see the seams where the pieces meet.

"*What* are you doing, Easnadh?" Jaxon stares at me as I bunch the sleeve of my sweater over my right hand.

"Punching through the sky," I say calmly. Dram, on the branch a few feet away from me, sends me an encouraging look. "Cover your heads," I add. And I haul back and slam my fist through the panel.

That was the idea, anyway. I imagined the surface shattering and firing sparkly shards of glass in every direction. What actually happens is less dramatic but much better. The panel pops up as easily as lifting a lid off a shoebox.

I turn to Dram with a triumphant grin. Because when the panel settles back down, it's no longer in alignment with the four surrounding panels. There's a little gap at one corner. I stick my hand in the space and slide the panel sideways.

"We did it!" My words of victory come out as a swish, not a shout. I'm not sure what—or who —might be on the other side of the ceiling panels.

Dram edges toward me along the branch, sliding his feet carefully sideways and keeping one hand on the tree trunk. Our eyes meet and we nod, knowing what has to happen next and what part we'll each play. While Royaltee holds Dram steady, Dram crouches down and encircles my legs with one arm. With a tight grip he hoists me into the air, higher and higher, while my stomach clenches and I warn myself not to look down. As I rise, I shove the loose panel firmly to the side. A dark gap meets me and slowly engulfs me. When my head and shoulders are above the level of the ceiling, I reach out and grab hold of one of the neighboring panels. Just as Dram gives me a quick upward bounce, I lean toward the edge of the gap and haul myself up.

I'm in.

A quick glance around doesn't give me much information. The space, which must extend over the top of the entire TimeTilter, is vast but dimly lit. A crisscrossing network of metal walkways and platforms is suspended from the true ceiling of the building. There are miles of shiny pipes and color-coded wires. There are hundreds of panels with blinking rows of digits and data. The TimeTilter environment that I've just left behind was both bizarre and beautiful, but to me this attic is even more fascinating: it's the brain and heart of the place.

But that little glimpse is all I have time for. I swivel and extend my hand, giving what help I can to Delia, Dram, Royaltee and finally Jaxon as they follow me up one by one.

As Jaxon pulls his feet in, I give an immense inward sigh that all of us—all the humans, that is—have made it safely. At the same moment, like he's reading my mind, Dublin gives a reverberating bark from below.

I peer back down at Dublin, who is still firmly encased in his sling. "Shhh. It's okay, boy," I tell him. "You're next."

Dram is holding the vine that's attached to both ends of the sling. He starts pulling, keeping it slow and steady, bringing Dublin up inch by inch.

Dublin wags as he nears us and his mouth opens to let out another happy bark.

That's my last view of him as the vine breaks with an angry pop that hits me like a bullet.

I scream out Dublin's name and reach out as if I could grab him. Only Dram's hold on my arm keeps me from rolling out and falling, falling, falling after Dublin, down and out of sight.

Chapter 5
Monet

As Monet backed her car out of its parking spot, her head was so full of theories that all she could think about was getting home as quickly as possible to sort through the mess. She had no attention to spare for anything else. So when she heard a solid and sickening thunk, she was instantly certain that she'd run smack into another car—or worse, another person.

She hit the brakes hard and whirled around to assess the damage.

It was, in fact, a person. A woman. But she was upright and looked neither broken nor bloodied. Before Monet could move, the woman walked right up to the driver's side window and drummed on the glass.

Monet put the car in park and rolled down the window. The woman bent over awkwardly to meet Monet eye to eye. Monet stammered the beginnings of an apology but the woman held up her hand.

"I've been looking for you," the woman said. "You seem to have been dashing all about today."

Intense eyes. Tall stature. Sleek hair in a low bun. Of course. Up close, Monet knew exactly who this was.

"Angelie...um, I mean, Dr. Bonneville," Monet said hesitantly. "I'm so sorry, I didn't see—"

"Angelie is fine. So, I've found you." Angelie gave a dim smile. "I know you have quite a few questions. Let's get you some answers, shall we?" She walked around the front of Monet's car, opened the passenger side door and slid smoothly into the seat.

Monet was uncomfortably aware that her mouth was hanging open in astonishment. She tried to speak but couldn't put together a string of logical words. She definitely wasn't giving a very good impression of herself as Collusia's supposed rising-star environmental designer.

Angelie pointed toward the TimeTilter building. "Drive us over to the North entrance."

It occurred to Monet that she could refuse. She could order Angelie out of her car, drive away and leave all this mystery and weirdness behind.

Yeah, right. Monet composed a quick email to her sister in her head. *I think I'm about to go back inside the TimeTilter. I guess I'm not getting fired. But I'm not sure I'll be coming out alive.*

The drive was brief and silent. Neither of them said a thing as Monet, at Angelie's pointed instructions, parked close to the North entryway in a spot marked Reserved.

Monet followed Angelie out of the car and up to the door, which swung wide in front of them. Angelie hadn't used an ID card to open the locked door. So maybe one of those exaggerated rumors about secret wearable—or even implanted—ID chips was actually true. The door whooshed closed and latched itself with a tight snap that made Monet jump.

"Follow me." Angelie walked swiftly down hallway after hallway. Each one was deserted but held a hollow echo of the day's noise and motion, like a school that had emptied out after the last bell.

Angelie turned abruptly and another door opened as quickly as if it were jumping out of her way. Monet hesitated. She didn't belong here. A small plaque on the door displayed the Collusia Confidential symbol: a closed eye ringed by two mirror-image letter Cs. This was a high security area. According to another round of rumors that Monet had always laughed at, one employee who tried to enter this area without clearance was not only fired but also never heard from again. His whole identity simply disappeared. Suddenly that story didn't seem so funny. But Angelie waved Monet in and she managed to cross the threshold without being vaporized.

They crossed a crowded lab to an office that was actually a bit of a disappointment. The wood floor was polished to a magnificent glossy shine, but the pale blue walls and the orderly line-up of chairs along one wall gave the whole place the effect of a slightly depressing waiting room. The only bright spots were the photographs: each one showed off a different stunning scene from inside the TimeTilter. Monet recognized every landscape and could have named its exact coordinates. After all, she had designed them herself.

Angelie jabbed at a small square panel. Monet heard a whir and a click that seemed to come from the door. Another lock? And was it shutting other people out or holding Monet in? Neither option seemed encouraging. More taps from Angelie triggered another whir. Monet tracked the sound to an upper corner of the room, where a panel slid over the lens of the security camera that was mounted there. Monet's throat tightened.

Angelie dragged two chairs to the center of the room, both facing the same way. She sank into one chair and signaled for Monet to sit next to her.

Perched on her seat, side-by-side with Angelie, Monet couldn't imagine what might be coming next. She reviewed the facts. Somehow Angelie had kept an eye on Monet throughout the day, which was definitely unsettling. Angelie would, of course, be aware that Monet's ID wasn't working and that she couldn't enter the TimeTilter. And Angelie knew that Monet had a lot of questions. So where were the answers she had promised? What were they doing in this nearly empty room?

Angelie pulled a remote control from one pocket and turned on a monitor that was mounted high on the wall. The screen faded from black to a photo of a teenage girl with big brown eyes and long hair in a middle part.

"Singer Sirtaine," Angelie said flatly. "Age fifteen. A runaway. She has the power of night vision."

It took Monet a moment to catch up to that last bit of information. "She has *what?*"

Angelie ignored her and clicked the remote to a fuzzy photo of a boy and a girl near a ramshackle house. "Jaxon Malley and Joy Binda, sixteen and fifteen. Foster children. Also runaways. Jaxon has telescopic vision. Joy has shared vision." Angelie flicked a quick glance toward Monet. "Which means she can project her sight over someone else's."

Click. An image of a broad-shouldered teenage boy and a little wild-eyed girl slid onto the monitor. Angelie's voice droned on. "Dram and Delia Moore. Ages fifteen and seven. Living in a train station. Dram now has the power of chrono vision. In other words, he can see the past. Delia: ultraviolet light perception."

One more click. Monet took in the image of a tall, ethereal girl with soft unfocused eyes.

Angelie took a deep breath. "Taylor—or rather, Royaltee. At the moment, she prefers to go by that one name. She's fourteen. Can you guess her power?"

An image of Hunter's document—the one with all the enhanced powers of vision—crashed back into Monet's memory. Angelie had mentioned five of the powers, but Monet couldn't recall the sixth. She shook her head mutely.

"She sees deep inside things," Angelie said, "to their fundamental composition. Microscopic vision."

Monet became aware that her body was shaking. She clenched her hands together in her lap. These photos, these names, these descriptions of extraordinary powers of sight—this deluge of data was not answering anything. It was, instead, drowning Monet in information that she absolutely could not sort through.

"Monet, pull yourself together, please. I need you to listen very carefully." Angelie's chair scraped along the polished wood floor as she pivoted to face Monet. "I wanted you to meet these children first. To see who they are. They all have something in common. I think you know what that is."

Maybe it should have been obvious but Monet's brain had called a halt to processing. She was a fly trapped on a sticky web, unable to move or look away.

"You've been denied access to the TimeTilter. Who do you think is in there?" Angelie's voice had turned harsh, like she was trying to jolt Monet out of her stillness and confusion. "All six of them. All under the influence of the superzeitgeber. Traveling their perception paths. For a very long time now."

"But...no," Monet said haltingly. "They shouldn't be in there. The site isn't ready. It's not open to the public. Not for another year, at least."

"You're quite right," Angelie broke in. "I know that better than anyone." She paused and ran both palms roughly across her cheeks, like she was sweeping out some ugly thoughts. "But that's the point. Don't you see? The superzeitgeber had to be tested. On someone."

"What do you mean, it had to be tested? The FDA approved it—or, at least, the approval is pending." Monet was sure of that fact, at least.

But Angelie shook her head. "That was a lie. Collusia bypassed the approval process. I don't know how."

"You can't be serious. What...exactly...is going on in there?" Monet couldn't keep her voice level. "What's happening to them?"

"It's an experiment, Monet. To test how long they can survive on a different perception path. To test how much superzeitgeber they can take."

Monet squeezed her eyes shut but the images of the six kids pulsed in front of her. None of this made sense. "Why?" She breathed the word out, over and over. "Why? *Why?*"

"I'll tell you what I was told." Angelie's voice dropped. Her words turned nearly pleading. "Because this is what humans always do, isn't it? Test the limits. Look for the extremes."

Monet opened her eyes and jerked back. "They're *children*. How could you let this—"

Angelie's answer came quickly. "This isn't...my vision. This isn't what I wanted. I had no choice."

Monet rose on unsteady feet and shook her head. "No choice? There's always a choice, Angelie. I don't know why you're going along with this but you have to end it. We have to get them out of there."

Angelie looked at her with sudden anguish.

"I respect you, Monet," Angelie said. "And I wish I wasn't dragging you into this with me. But believe me: I truly can't stop this."

"You can. You have to." Monet inhaled as deeply as she could. The air felt thin and foul in her lungs. "These children...they're being experimented on without their consent. Without anyone's consent. Can't you see where this is heading? When this...experiment...is over, what do you think? That they'll just be set free to tell the world what happened to them? There's no way they'll be allowed to walk away from all this."

Angelie stood to face Monet.

Seconds wound into minutes.

When Angelie spoke again, her voice was a nearly imperceptible breath. "I'm being watched. All the time. Why do you think I brought you here? I was told you would be the next...subject...to go into the TimeTilter."

Monet went still.

"I told you. I have no choice." Angelie's intense eyes barely blinked. "But maybe you're right. Maybe...you do."

Angelie stepped back. She kept her voice low but talked fast, her words stumbling over each other as if she wasn't sure what would come out next. "I'm going to give you a short head start. That's all I can do. And when that moment comes, you'll have two choices about what you're going to do from here." Angelie held up one finger. "One: You could enter the TimeTilter. I won't prep you with the superzeitgeber, so your presence will merge all perception paths. You'll be able find the children and pull them out. But I will tell you this. There *is* an exit problem. Taking these children out of here now, with their systems full of superzeitgeber...that will be...dangerous. And permanent. So..." Angelie held up a second finger. "Two: You could run. Get out of here. Try to get help. But...I'll be frank about that option too. Someone will see you go. And the children will probably be gone before you get back. Along with any evidence of what we've been doing."

Monet's heart thumped. That was all she could feel. The accelerating beat filled her chest and her gut and her head.

Angelie took hold of her shoulders. Up close again, Monet was sure she saw something there. Something in Angelie's eyes. A flicker, quick as a hummingbird's wing and then gone. Monet took a chance.

"Help me," Monet said.

Angelie swung her around and guided her to the door. She clicked three keys on the pad and pulled the door wide open.

"I'll tell you what you should do," Angelie said. "Run."

Chapter 6
Singer

I've screamed my throat hoarse but that doesn't bring Dublin back.

I would have jumped after him. I would have. Only Dram's unbreakable hold keeps me here in the TimeTilter's attic.

Jaxon comes up to me and puts his hands on my shoulders. "Good-bye, Easnadh," he says. I believe, at first, that he's going to pull me loose from Dram's grip and let me go. But that doesn't happen. Instead, Jaxon gives me a light hug and steps away. He backs up to the gap where we pushed aside the panel, kneels and starts to lower himself down.

"Jaxon, don't—" My voice comes out thin and scratchy but Jaxon hears me and pauses.

"I'll look for Dublin. I promise that. I'll help him if I can." Jaxon's mouth, usually so quick to smile, is set in a resolute line. "But that's not the only reason I have to go, Singer. I've let Joy down too many times. I'm not leaving her behind."

"I'm going with you."

"You're not," Jaxon says. "You have to go on. Keep moving forward. You're pretty amazing at that, you know. You've never given up."

"How...how will you even find Joy?" I choke the words out.

"I don't know. I really don't. We won't be in the same perception." Jaxon sighs. "I just know I can't leave her. I have to try."

"Jaxon is right," Dram says. He drops his hold around my waist and takes my hand. "We need you, Singer. We have to get out of here. I can't do that alone."

I see now that Jaxon has looped and knotted a vine around his waist. The other end is tied to one of the walkway railings. Jaxon gives the vine a quick tug to test it and then drops.

Dram and I scramble to the edge of the gap and look down. The vine swings loosely above the highest branch. Jaxon is gone, really and truly gone, out of sight and perception.

It make me sick—leaves me literally retching—to look down the long craggy lines of the tree and imagine Dublin falling that distance. Dram hears my agonized noises and sees my twisted face and does me the kindness of pulling me away again and sliding the loose panel over the gap. I sit down and curl up with my arms around my bent knees.

Delia sidesteps her way over. She sits next to me, pushing her small shoulder up against my mine. It's sweet and sad at the same time. It reminds me that I'm not the only one around here who's scared and despairing. I put one arm around Delia and then lay my head gently on top of hers. Her whole body is shaking.

"Dram," I say softly. His back is turned to me and he doesn't respond, so I call his name again. His head whips around.

"Come over here," he says. "Alone."

His tone is so dire that I move right away. I take Delia's hand, thinking she'd feel better if she sticks with me, but Dram shakes his head and slices his hand in a decisive motion that says "no." It turns out Delia is not moving anyway. Her eyes are closed and she's rooted to her spot.

"I'll be right back," I tell her.

When I reach Dram's side, he's staring at a grid of skinny silver pipes that all come from a single tank. Dram leans forward and brushes a finger along a bunch of numbers and letters that are etched on the side of the tank. He stops when he reaches three of the letters. SZG. He traces each one carefully.

I tilt my head and raise my eyebrows. "SZG for superzeitgeber?"

"Maybe," Dram says.

"So?"

"Look how the pipes all feed down into the TimeTilter." Dram points along the path of the nearest pipe. "So they store the stuff here. And I guess they can control the flow or whatever. But it's not *released* up here."

I get it. This attic is a storage area. And also a work area. Which means...if people need to be in here to adjust and maintain things, they can't be exposed to the superzeitgeber while they're working. Which also means...right now, *we're* not exposed to the superzeitgeber any more.

I remember exactly what Dram once told us about leaving the TimeTilter. That there could be—

"An exit problem." Royaltee finishes my thought. I don't know when she joined Dram and me but she's right on top of the conversation. Her voice is quiet and unfamiliar; I realize that I've barely heard her speak since we met. But she has more to say now. She takes a resolute breath and says, "We've been under the superzeitgeber's influence for a long time. Some of us longer than others. Coming out of it isn't going to be easy. Especially for Delia."

Royaltee turns and points back at where Delia is sitting, exactly where I left her.

Dram takes one quick look at her and bolts. He's by Delia's side in two seconds. Royaltee and I rush after him and crouch down. The look on Delia's face makes my insides twist. Her eyes are still closed but tears slide down her checks like blood from a wound. Her whole body vibrates but not from cold or fear. Some sort of horrible tremor is making her shake and twitch.

"We're next," Royaltee says.

Dram stares at Delia, frozen. I can guess what he's thinking: that he let her down. That he hasn't looked out for her. That he's not good enough, as a big brother or anything else. I feel his heartache so deeply that I have to look away.

If Royaltee is right, we don't have much time. We have to find help before it's too late for Delia and too late for the rest of us. I turn to Royaltee. "I'm going on that walkway. You go the other way. Look for any way out. Any door, any gap, anything."

My fatigue hasn't faded. I still feel a bone-melting weariness. But I shove it out of the way, trying to fill that space with any scraps of determination I can find. I make my way along the walkway as fast as I can, though it's no more than one halting step after another. That makes me think of Dublin after his injury. When he ran, he tucked in his tail and got low to the ground and was still convinced he was the speediest dog on the planet. I shake off the memory. The walkway sways the tiniest bit under my movement but I keep going.

With a quick glance over my shoulder, I see Royaltee racing away. She skids right, then left, then right again—I have no idea if she's following some kind of pattern or not, but it doesn't matter.

She is filled with urgency and covering ground fast.

I turn back to my own search. The few spotlights that are scattered here and there cast a strange sort of light, illuminating some sections of the attic and leaving others in dusty dimness that makes it hard to see distinctly. But there's one thing I can't miss. This walkway that I'm on is slowly rising. It's subtle but real. The ceiling is getting closer.

This is something good.

I think.

I take a chance and scream "Over here!" as loudly as I can.

There's a brief and complete silence. Then I hear the swelling sound of footsteps clanging along the walkway. First Royaltee appears, then Dram with Delia curled in his arms. I watch them as they move in and out of the spotlights in a freeze-frame race toward me. The sight of them propels me forward like I'm caught in the path of an ocean wave.

We surge on. Dram gasps under Delia's weight but never slows. As the walkway widens he moves to one side of me and Royaltee slides in to my other side, each offering me their support. The walkway isn't just getting wider; it's rising more steeply now, the angle of ascent increasing until we finally reach another platform. From here, there's a staircase of ten steps leading to a trapdoor in the ceiling.

I look back one more time. The TimeTilter attic spreads out north, south, east and west as if it goes on forever. That's how it felt to be in there: like forever.

Time to bring this to an end.

As Delia whimpers and moans, we all give the trapdoor a shove and it opens without a fight. I remember how Joy kicked and punched at the East Portal when we first entered the TimeTilter. I remember her fierce and focused energy, and I hope that she can call on it now, wherever she is. I remember Jaxon's courage when he turned back after nearly escaping with us. And I remember Dublin, my sweet Dublin, who was my constant steady friend and somehow isn't here by my side to take these last steps with me.

As we surge to the roof, the bold and unforgiving sunshine nearly knocks us down.

It's daytime, I can see that.

A regular blue sky. White clouds. The colors look muted and hazy, as if my eyes aren't working quite right.

What day is it? We perceived nearly three days, I think, in the TimeTilter. But that time must have been measured in hours out here.

My brain is starting to feel fuzzy.

I try to keep it together.

Still arm in arm, we stagger across the flat roof toward the closest edge. And then I finally know for sure that I'm bending toward a superzeitgeber exit hallucination because what I see is a young woman running barefoot on a dirt road with three security guards behind her and gaining fast and from the expression on her face there's no doubt that she's running for her life.

Chapter 7
Monet

Monet was not a runner.

Walks in the park, hikes with her sister, strolls through the city: these things were good. She needed time to observe the smallest details. A single wind-blown leaf skittering ahead of her like a tiny ship at sea. A weed fighting for a roothold in a concrete crack. Slabs of fungus spiraling up a tree trunk like a staircase.

But now, Monet ran.

Angelie had given her a head start, a small one. Monet took it and bolted from the room. She skidded sideways and pounded down hallways that all looked alike—silent and grey—with her breath coming in useless puffs. She felt hands grasping at her though no one was there, heard the shriek of an alarm that never rang, let out a shattered cry that never left her lips. She pounded at three different doors before she found one that gave in and released her from the building.

Monet ran with her heart in her throat and with her eyes wide.

She sprinted around a corner, across a small parking lot and down a dirt road that paralleled the north wall of the TimeTilter. In her panic Monet could not be sure but she guessed and hoped and had to believe that this road looped back around to the entrance where she had parked her car.

Monet's soft clogs, which she had always considered the most comfortable shoes on the planet, were not made for speed. She kicked them off as she hurtled forward, sending the shoes in a tumbling arc into the weeds.

She ran until her own momentum lurched her forward onto her hands.

When she rose, her head start was over.

She looked over her shoulder just long enough to see three security guards burst from a tree line about five hundred feet behind her and start their pursuit.

If she could outrun them, if she could ignore the fire in her lungs and legs, then maybe she could reach her car and blast out of here and make it to safety and get help.

If not...

If not...was there another path? At maybe a dozen spots along this north side of the TimeTilter, skinny metal maintenance ladders were mounted on the wall. If Monet climbed one of them and got onto the roof...well, she knew every trapdoor into the attic. She could drop into the TimeTilter and find the kids and maybe break them free.

Still bolting along the dirt road, Monet stole a quick look up the next ladder.

There, at the top. Someone was up there.

Four faces.

Four teens. She knew them instantly. They looked at her and tracked her motion and exuded such intense fear and confusion that she could feel the emotions surging from here.

They were making their own break for freedom.

So there was only one thing she could do. Only one action she could take to save these children.

She did not take the ladder.

She shouted at the guards, pulling their attention to her.

And she ran.

Chapter 8
Singer

I watch as Royaltee half climbs and half slides down the ladder. Dram is right behind her, struggling from rung to rung with Delia slung over his shoulders in a firefighter's carry.

As Dram descends, I turn around to back down the ladder myself.

That's when I see the smoke. At first, it's no more than a tendril rising sleepily from the rooftop. But within seconds the smoke billows out into a dense dark cloud that's lit from below with a vivid orange glow.

I understand with complete and devastating clarity that this smoke means fire. Somewhere in the bowels of the TimeTilter, a fire is burning.

In the flicker of a second my mind takes me back to the salvage yard, waking up in the busted-up Chevy Malibu ringed by flames. With the image come all the emotions and fears that rocked through me back then. That I was nobody. That I was always falling short of perfect. Not worth a picture on a wall. Living in a house that was never my home.

Then something happened that I couldn't have imagined. Jaxon looked point-blank at me, saw me at the most vulnerable place I have ever been when the superzeitgeber overwhelmed me, and yet he refused to leave me behind. Dram gave me his trust and held my secrets and shared my hope—before we ever laid eyes on each other. Even Royaltee followed my lead; with her ability to see deep into the inner structure of things, somehow she spotted something of value in me.

And Angelie...what had she said? "You're exactly the person I've been looking for." She must have seen something I never knew was there.

There's a point to rounding all these thoughts up in my head. They're the fuel I need to move forward again. To take the next step. And that step will not mean following Dram, Delia and Royaltee down the ladder.

Because now, even now as superzeitgeber drains from my body and leaves me hazy and hobbled, I know this: I am strong enough to keep fighting.

I look down at Dram, who has made it nearly to the bottom. At the moment when his foot is about to touch the ground, he looks up and sees my face and freezes. His eyes narrow. He knows.

This must be how Jaxon felt the last time he saw Joy.

Doing what feels right and good in your heart can still nearly break you.

I reach an arm toward Dram as if I could brush his cheek with my fingers.

Then I turn and head back into the fire.

Chapter 9
Joy

I am Joy.

I am alone.

I don't know where I am.

No, that's not right—I know exactly *where* I am: I'm standing with my back against a moss-patched rock and staring at a snapping wall of fire.

The problem is this: I don't know *when* I am.

I left Jaxon without a word. Left him with no last wave or warning. And the second—the very second—I was out of his sight, my time ripped away from his, as neatly as a piece of paper torn in two.

I chose my own time path. I was pulled out of here and thrown back in again.

I've been alone for what feels like forever. Jaxon and I, we're long out of step.

I wonder if Jaxon could be beside me right now: at the same place but in a different hour, leaving us time blind to each other. I reach out my hand and imagine Jaxon doing the same, his fingertips materializing as they touch mine.

But all I see are the flames jostling closer, and all I feel is the air warming me past comfort.

I won't try to put out the fire. After all, I know who started it. As sure as I've ever been of anything, I'm sure of this: Jaxon did this. He found a way to set the TimeTilter on fire. He found a way to build this blazing beacon and draw me in. To merge our perceptions again.

I move one pace closer to the wildfire. At any moment, Jaxon will move into my path and sight. I won't have to be alone. He'll offer me his hand and his help and I'll take it. I'm so certain of this that when a figure really does appear in front of me I start to say his name.

It isn't Jaxon.

I never thought it could be Singer. She's the one who I thought would hold us back and would need rescuing. Yet here she is, her body battered, her spirit bold. She half staggers and half swaggers forward through the smoke.

I never expected to see her again. I never expected to be so relieved to see her again.

I step toward her but before my foot hits the ground, I catch sight of two streaks of red fire. The first streak is a fragment of burning wood that's shooting from the flames and on a path to connect with me. But the second streak is the solid body of a red-gold dog who knocks me three feet back and saves my life.

When I catch my breath and get to my feet, Singer is on one side of me and Dublin the red-gold dog is on the other. Together they drag and hoist me along a path that I suddenly realize is getting closer to the fire. I pull back but Singer shakes her head at me, her throat too dry and hoarse to talk. She points to a pile of fallen branches that's way too close to the smoke and heat and then she chokes out the one name I've been dreaming of saying: Jaxon.

I shake off Singer and her dog and lurch toward the cracked and smoldering heap of forest debris. Jaxon is under there, trapped. That's what Singer was trying to tell me.

I ignore my soaring pain and the spreading fire and let instinct take over.

A roundhouse kick and another and another.

A jab and a right cross and a front kick and a sweep.

I fight that pile of rubble like it's my worst enemy. I throw every move I know against it.

Just ahead of the flames, I crumble the pile to bits. My battered hands find Jaxon and pull him free.

The four of us turn away from the fire that brought us together. As the TimeTilter burns, we head toward an exit and an ending that not even our super powers of sight can help us see.

Chapter 10
Singer

I'm not sure of time. I'm not sure of my perceptions. But this is what I remember.

With Dublin—my bruised and battered but gloriously alive Dublin—leading the way, we raced to stay ahead of the fire. But it surged toward us faster than we could travel, and we swerved wide to stay out of its path. We hunched in a ditch with a low rush of water that glowed bright yellow—or maybe that was only a reflection of the flames.

That's what kept us alive, I think.

When the crackle and roar subsided we came up out of the ditch and couldn't believe our eyes. The fire had burned a charred path to an outer wall of the TimeTilter. It had met that wall and devoured a chunk of it, leaving a gaping hole with edges that still smoldered as the fire rampaged on.

We rushed to that wall as fast as our singed and fractured bodies could go. We burst through the gap without caring what might be on the other side. We plunged back into the pace of ordinary time like stones skipping across a pond, smacking the surface over and over again until we sank.

I looked back once and saw that we weren't the only ones escaping. The black shadows poured out of the gap in our wake. They were more than shadows, now. They looked as solid as me. But maybe that part wasn't real.

What happened next sent quivers of alarm up the back of my neck.

Even in my superzeitgeber-exit-problem state of hallucination, I knew it was all wrong to see Angelie here. She loomed tall, her face stretched tight with what looked like panic. She picked up Joy and Jaxon—one in each arm—as easily as lifting pillows and put them in the back of a long grey van. Then it was my turn and Dublin's. I didn't have the awareness or sense to resist. In the van I thought my eyes must be closed and my mind must be dreaming because there was Dram with Delia gathered against him. I tried to reach my hand out to him but I don't think I moved. Angelie climbed in after us, holding Royaltee and staring down at her with heartbreak in her eyes.

Then Angelie put something over her face, something that in my muddied mind looked like the scuba mask that deep-sea divers wear.

The air changed.

It tasted thick as pudding and I could hardly breathe it in.

That's where the memories end.

The room I'm in now—this room that I don't remember entering—

is not much bigger than the van. It's a tight windowless space that feels like a forgotten closet. But it's bright with fluorescent light, so I can see that we're all here: Dublin, Dram, Delia, Jaxon, Joy, Royaltee and Angelie.

There are three things that I notice right away.

One is that I feel like the superzeitgeber has been knocked right out of me. I'm kind of shaky, the way I feel when a bad migraine headache has passed. But the little jolty hiccups in my sight are gone, and I don't feel so crazily thirsty anymore. The colors around me—the blue of my jeans, the orangey red of Dublin's fur, the pea-green of the chair cushion—all look the way I remember them, without that supersaturated glare.

The second thing is that Royaltee is still pressed tight against Angelie. I can't figure that one out so for now I let it go.

And the third thing is that there are two people here who I've never seen before. One is a young woman who sits lightly on the edge of her chair and tracks Angelie's every twitch with suspicious eyes. The other is a tall man who slouches in his chair and keeps pushing up the drooping sleeves of his blue button-down shirt.

We all stare at each other, like this is some awkward social gathering, until Joy breaks the silence. "You said we could go when this was over." She tilts her chin in a challenge to Angelie. "So start talking or we're walking."

Angelie returns Joy's look unswervingly. "You're right, Joy. It's time for real answers." Angelie takes a moment to meet our gazes, each of us one by one. Then she stands and, in a way that's unnervingly familiar, starts to pace back and forth—as much as she can in this little space—as she talks.

"Dram," Angelie points at him, "came to before the rest of you. He told me a bit about what you discovered. So, first of all: yes, the TimeTilter has an exit problem. The superzeitgeber was quite experimental. We still don't know how long anyone can be under its influence without permanent effects."

"*Permanent* effects? Such as what?" The young woman's voice nearly crackles with anger.

Angelie meets her gaze calmly. "Disorientation, Monet. An inability to function in regular time." The young woman—Monet—looks like she's ready to boil over but Angelie holds up her hand. "Let me go on." She gestures toward the slouchy man. "That's why Hunter and I have started working—completely on our own—on an antidote to reverse those effects."

Delia raises her hand like she's in a school classroom. I wonder how much of this she's taking in. Out of all of us, her exit from the TimeTilter was the hardest. While so many things seem foggy, Delia's blank face and ragged moans in the TimeTilter attic are never going to fade. Angelie lets a tiny smile tug at her lips and gives Delia a nod.

"Can we have that, please?" Delia says. "The anti-thing?"

"You have, in fact, had the antidote. All five of you." Angelie glances at Hunter, who sits higher in his chair and takes over.

"Um, yes, you've had the antidote. And, well, as to whether it works, I would say, look at you." He waves a hand at us in a way that I think is meant to be encouraging. "Now, um, I will be honest. We—Angelie and I, that is—we don't know if this reversal is going to, um, last. But I think, well, I would say this: so far, so good." He hikes up his shirtsleeves one more time. I notice that he seems to be avoiding Monet's gaze.

Dram draws Delia even closer to him. "You have been playing with our lives," he says.

I put my hand over Dram's. I say to Angelie, as simply and as fiercely as I can, "I hope Jaxon's fire burned the TimeTilter to the ground."

Angelie looks at me with round eyes. Jaxon has exactly the same expression on his face.

"Jaxon didn't start it," Angelie says slowly. "I thought you knew. Hunter and I, then Monet, then all of you—we were figuring out too much. The shivelers started the fire to burn down the TimeTilter. To bury its secrets." She looks toward Royaltee and her voice turns so indistinct that I can barely hear her. "You were all meant to disappear in that fire."

I latch on one thing out of about a zillion that I don't understand right now. "What are shivelers?"

Then every one of us starts pelting so many words at Angelie that it sounds like ricocheting gunfire. Angelie drops into a chair and bends her head into her hands. This is the first time I've ever seen her rattled.

Hunter shifts and waves his arms again, trying to quiet us. He looks at the young woman. "Monet, um, I hope that you can forgive me. I wanted, well, *really* wanted to tell you all of this before. I wanted to ask you to join our...um, what should I call it? Our research. Our resistance. But...I'll let Angelie explain it from the beginning."

Angelie raises her head and sighs. Then she tells us everything.

"You've all heard me say this," she begins, back to pacing again. "The TimeTilter is only a small part of Collusia. This company has irons in a lot of different fires, so to speak. Collusia researches everything from bioengineering to sustainability to construction. So many projects are underway, yet each department keeps its research very secret. In fact, when I was hired here to continue my work on the superzeitgeber, I was specifically instructed not to talk about my research or share my results with anyone else at Collusia. There is simply no communication or collaboration across our departments. You've seen that yourself, Monet. And it always struck me as odd."

Angelie takes a quick breath and smooths her hair back from her cheeks. "To be honest, I was resentful, too, that Collusia had bought out my company and fired so many of my employees. So I started to do some investigating. Some very deep investigating. I soon realized that every project was connected to one person: Lisa Solein. If that name sounds familiar to any of you, it should. She's the founder and CEO of Collusia. Her name is in the news all the time because of a few flashy projects that Lisa lets the public know about. But the real work that's happening here—that, of course, is all secret. All behind the scenes. I kept digging into those secret projects and barely believed what I was finding. I needed help processing it all, and that's when I recruited Hunter to help me."

Angelie folds back into her seat and Hunter takes up the story.

"Well, um, it took some time. But we discovered the true purpose of Lisa's work. The true purpose of every project. It is, well, let me tell you, it is surprising. Lisa is preparing herself to survive the end of the...um...the world."

Hunter's delivery is so low key that no one reacts. It's like we're all holding our breath until we see where this is going.

"The TimeTilter...well, it was never meant for gamers," he continues. "That was, um, definitely a ruse to raise money for Lisa's research. The TimeTilter is, um, preposterous though it sounds, it's a testing ground."

"A place to test the superzeitgeber, of course," Angelie chimes back in. "Lisa wants to use the superzeitgeber to give herself more time. Not, of course, perceived time. That's pretty much all the superzeitgeber can deliver right now. What she was aiming for was...well, you might guess where this is heading. She wants the superzeitgeber to create more *real* time."

Hunter tugs on his shirtsleeves for the hundredth time. "Which I, um, admit, at first thought was interesting. And worthy. But it's not...no, obviously now I can see it's not at all worthy the way Lisa plans to use that time." Hunter still isn't meeting Monet's eyes, but he keeps plowing on. "Lisa plans to be one of the few to live through any disaster that hits our, you know, our planet. Along with a small group of people she thinks are worthy enough to survive with her. And she...it's difficult to believe this part...she wants to use the superzeitgeber time to, um, make herself the most powerful person to survive. To rule what's left of the world. Which is, well, the only word I can come up with is...outlandish. But then, I suppose, in Lisa's *perception*...no pun intended...she might be thinking, um, go big or go home."

"Indeed," says Angelie. "Of course, she wanted to give herself whatever advantages she could. That was the point of experimenting with your vision. She was testing different ways of enhancing sight, to see what might give her the greatest edge."

I catch sight of Monet's face. Her eyes have turned icier. "You two act like this is all Lisa Solein's work," she says. "But *you*, Angelie, you've been part of it. You kidnapped these kids. You messed with their eyes. You threw them in the TimeTilter. You tried to stop *me* from helping them. I told you how this would end. Lisa will be looking for them. Their *lives* are in danger now. How can you pretend that you're not as horrible as Lisa is?"

We all blink and sit back when Royaltee, who has been so silent and still, rises from her seat and strides to Angelie's side. She looks up at Angelie and takes hold of her hand. "Tell them," she says.

Angelie begins to speak but stops, her lips pinched together. Whatever she meant to say, I think she's too choked up to let it out.

"I'll tell them, then. Not the whole story, but the most important parts," Royaltee says. She squeezes Angelie's hand. "My real name is Taylor, and I used to be Angelie's daughter."

I can't help it. I actually laugh. It's the kind of laugh that happens when something is not at all funny but so over the top that your brain doesn't want to accept it. Royaltee looks my way but seems to understand that I'm not being mean.

"Not her biological daughter. Her foster daughter. For just a little while when I was younger," Royaltee says. "Until Angelie had to move out of state. And I had to stay behind."

It's kind of tough to watch Royaltee look up at Angelie with so much loss and love. Angelie's face sends the same message back. With one finger she traces the path of a shooting star that's stitched on the sleeve of Royaltee's sweater.

"So," Royaltee says with a hitch of her shoulders. "I got placed in the commune. But Angelie...she never stopped looking for a way to get me back. The thing is...Lisa found me first."

Now it's Royaltee's turn to get choked up. Angelie rubs her shoulder and picks up the story. "I don't know how Lisa found out about her. But she did. And she put Royaltee into the TimeTilter."

Royaltee gives a single pained nod. "Lisa said she'd...kill all of us...if I told any of you the truth."

"Finding Royaltee—that was a powerful move by Lisa," Angelie says. "She knew I was learning too much. And she bought my silence very easily. She gave me the task of finding five more subjects to put into the TimeTilter. And if I told anyone what she was doing, she threatened she would pull Royaltee from the TimeTilter so quickly that she would never be able to function in real time again."

"Which, um, is why...as you can imagine," Hunter says, "why we knew we had to come up with the antidote."

I'm beginning, dubiously, to put this all together. Angelie's hidden message, from what feels like so long ago, plays again in my head: *If you think there's something strange about how I found you, you are right. If you think there's something strange about the fire and the explosion, you are right. There is more to the TimeTilter than a game. And there is more to Collusia than the TimeTilter.*

That has turned out to be an understatement.

I raise a tentative hand, just like Delia did. "One thing you still haven't told us." I pause, because I'm not quite sure I want to hear the answer. "What are shivelers?"

"An excellent question, Singer," Angelie says, though her resigned face tells me she wishes I hadn't asked it again. "Shivelers are... there's no way to make this seem reasonable...they are short-term time travelers. That's what Lisa calls them, anyway. They don't actually travel through time. They travel around the TimeTilter and try to intercept your perceptions."

"That's a pretty way of putting it," Joy says, her voice full of acid. "What they did to us, though. That was ugly."

"Are they real?" Delia's high voice pipes up again. I try to imagine all this conversation from her perspective. It seems like perfect material for nightmares.

Hunter leans forward and pats Delia's arm. "They, um, I know they look like shadows. But they are real people. Very real. It's just, well, when they cross your path a second before or after you, it feels exactly like...um, well I've never felt it so I don't know exactly..."

"I'll fill you in," Joy says. "It feels like someone is passing through your body. And it hurts."

"I'm sorry you went through that," Angelie says. I realize it's the first time she's apologized for any of this. "I knew Lisa was recruiting some Collusia employees to act as shivelers. I don't think they had any idea what they were doing. And until I saw them coming out of the TimeTilter during the fire, I didn't even realize they were already in there."

"I saw them coming out of the TimeTilter too," Monet says. Her coldness toward Angelie has lifted a tiny bit. "They were wearing something that looked like armor, I think. With gas masks."

"Yes, um, exactly," Hunter answers. "It *is* some sort of armor.

Something that lets the shivelers—and Lisa too, of course—survive just about any condition, um, inside the TimeTilter. Or, if I may say it without being too dramatic, survive just about any condition that might happen at the end of...um...the world."

"If you're sure about all this," Jaxon pipes up, "why don't you tell someone about this? Someone who can stop her?"

"Because there is one very critical thing I don't know," Angelie says. "I think, maybe, that Lisa put other...subjects...into the TimeTilter. I'm not sure of it. And if they exist, I don't know where they are. But I do know what Lisa would do to them if she felt threatened. If she found out that all her secrets had been exposed. She would ki—" Angelie glances at Delia. "Well, perhaps I don't have to spell it out."

I'm more tired than I realize because I have to close my eyes for a minute. When I open them, things take another surreal turn.

Angelie leaves the room. She's gone for only a minute. When she comes back in, I shiver. I'm getting a razor-sharp flashback to being inside the TimeTilter, because she's dressed in body-skimming armor that makes her look exactly like the shivelers that attacked us in the marsh—only more substantial than shadowy.

"We do, um, have this one thing on our side." Hunter offers a grin that no one is ready to return. "It's a prototype of the armor."

"We got hold of this by means that were, obviously, dangerous. And illegal," Angelie says. "But having the armor...all I can say is this: it gives us a chance."

Us? Gives *us* a chance to do what?

I didn't say it out loud but Angelie sees the lack of comprehension in our faces.

"I know most of you didn't come here by choice," Angelie says. "But, as Monet said, Lisa will be looking for all of us now. To stop us. To make sure we don't share her secrets. If you join me...I think, with all of us fighting against Collusia together, we could do this. We could bring Lisa down. Before she hurts anyone else."

"How?" My voice is loud and decisive now.

"We go underground," Angelie answers. She smiles at Delia's confused face. "No, Delia, not literally. I mean that we go into hiding. And we keep digging into what Lisa is doing. We keep researching the antidote to the superzeitgeber. We study this armor and make our own version."

"Make our own? Why waste time with that? Do you want to rule the world too?" Monet says. She squares her shoulders as if she's ready to take Angelie down again.

"No," Angelie shoots back. "If we improve the armor, we can protect ourselves from Lisa—but it's not just for us. We'll do something different. We'll take all this technology, all these advances that Lisa wants to use to make herself more powerful—and we'll do something better. We'll use the armor to protect ourselves while we search for anyone else Lisa might have put in the TimeTilter. And imagine if a disaster really strikes. Fires, earthquakes, tsunamis, droughts—this armor could keep people safe. We'll use our work to help all the people that Lisa thinks aren't worth saving. Because they are." Angelie looks at me. "Every one of them."

I tangle my fingers in Dublin's fur. He bumps against me and lifts a paw onto my leg. His coat is scruffy, muddy and worn.

As for me, I might have just a little bit of superzeitgeber left inside because, throughout all this talk, I sometimes felt that I was on a different perception path than Angelie and Hunter. Everything they said was supersaturated with glaring weirdness.

Dram turns to me and leans in, creating a brief one-on-one world for us that I'm incredibly grateful for, after everything Angelie and

Hunter have poured over us. Dram watches me steadily. He, at least, seems thoroughly here-and-now.

"You never told me," Dram says, "how Dublin survived that fall."

I grimace, thinking of Dublin plummeting down, out of our sight. "Jaxon told me that when he got to the bottom of the tree, Dublin was standing there waiting for him. The sling—the one we made from your jacket—was hanging near the ground with the vines tangled up in a branch. That must have broken the fall."

I stroke Dublin's rounded head and he stretches his nose toward me, trying to give my face a lick. Dublin has met more obstacles— more extremes—in the TimeTilter than in any competition he's ever faced. But his brown eyes are shining with a new energy.

Dram slides Delia onto his lap and moves closer to me. We breathe together, an inhale-exhale rhythm that we both try to slow down.

"What happens now?" he asks me.

"I don't know," I answer as truthfully as I can. "There's something in there, in what Angelie is saying. She did awful things but she wants to make it right." I sigh. "I think...I think I want to keep moving forward. To take the next step and fight—in case there's anyone else like us who needs saving."

"In that case, I think...I do too." Dram gives me a smile and a gentle shoulder nudge. "But—you have parents."

That's a point I can't ignore. However much I believe Mom and Dad wouldn't really miss me, I would never want to hurt them. But if everything that Angelie has said is true and Lisa will really be hunting for all of us, then going back would put my parents in danger too.

"It's only Saturday, right?" I say. "So, hopefully, they won't notice I'm missing for a couple more days. By that time, I'll figure out a way to let them know I'm okay."

I pull back to study Dram's face more carefully. "What about you? You and Delia left your foster home."

"Nobody is looking for us," he says matter-of-factly. "And anyway, I think we have sort of found a new home."

Dram looks around the tiny room at the rows of chairs and at the bare windowless walls. Gently he shifts Delia into my arms. He stands and pulls a small, pale blue leaf from his pocket. He props it up against the wall, and when he steps back I look at it more closely.

Someone—it must be Delia—has found a way to make a sketch on the leaf. It's a tiny portrait of a girl with long hair parted in the middle. She looks ahead with a determined and powerful stare.

"Delia drew it for me with a crayon she held on to," Dram says. He sits back next to me and puts one arm around my shoulders. "I had never laid eyes on you but somehow I knew exactly who you would be."

"Oh yeah? And who is that?" I ask with a smile.

"Someone," Dram says, "worth remembering."

To: [*Email group: redacted*]

Subject: DermAra

*IT'S TIME TO FACE THE **FIGHT AGAINST COLLUSIA** TOGETHER!*

RESISTERS: YOUR HELP IS DESPERATELY NEEDED.
WE ARE IMPLEMENTING THE NEXT PHASE OF OUR FIGHT..

*OUR GOAL: TO DESIGN **DERMARA**, OUR OWN BIO-ARMOR THAT WILL OUTLAST AND OUTPERFORM COLLUSIA'S TIMETILTER ARMOR.*

JOIN US. DO YOUR PART.

*YOU KNOW WHERE TO FIND US: GO TO **COLLUSIA.COM**. WHEN YOU GET THERE, USE THE PASSWORD (**STARFISH**) TO FIND YOUR WAY TO OUR HIDDEN SITE.*

TIME IS SHORT BUT THE RESISTANCE IS STRONG.

AB / DM / DM / HS / JB / JM / MJ / RB / SS / DUBLIN

TimeTilter

ABOUT THE AUTHOR

Sonia Ellis is the author of *Talk to Me*. She is a former chemical engineer who now haunts libraries, rescues stray dogs, and believes that every young person has the potential to save the world. Sonia lives in Massachusetts with two unruly dogs named Chase and Bleu.

ACKNOWLEDGMENTS

One of the most gratifying things about writing a book is this: it widens the circle of people who inspire you, hold your hand, and always seem to have your back. That's exactly what happened when I was lucky enough to join the spectacular team of Through My Window. There is no way to adequately express my appreciation for this amazing group of people, but here is a heartfelt attempt.

Thanks to Glenn Ellis, who always believed in me and never once doubted that I could do this; to Beth McGinnis-Cavanaugh, who put her entire heart and soul into this project from the start; to Al Rudnitsky, who truly inspired my imaginative education; and to Isabel Huff, whose spirit and creativity never cease to amaze me. And while I can't name all of you, my thanks to every Smith College and Springfield Technical Community College student who has contributed so passionately to Through My Window.

Thanks to Pendred Noyce and Barnas Monteith of Tumblehome Learning for their wonderful support, encouragement, and professional advice.

Thanks to Cicily Corbett, my fellow believer in story genius: You created a safe and cozy space to share our works in progress and provided consistently helpful insight.

Thanks to Andrea Beaghton, my sister: You designed a perfectly beautiful cover that brings to life exactly what was in my head and my heart for this story.

Thanks to Eli Bigelow, my BFOAT—where to begin and where to end? You helped me build a new world and kept the rest of life at bay while I finished this book.

And thanks to Jamie, my son: You lifted me out of some writerly depths of despair, listening and brainstorming at just the right moments.

This material is based upon work
supported by the
National Science Foundation under
Grant Nos. 1223868 and 1223460.
Any opinions, findings and
conclusions or recommendations
expressed in this material are those of
the author(s) and do not necessarily
reflect the views of the
National Science Foundation.